WALL STREET JOURNAL & USA TODAY BESTSELLING AUTHOR
SAPPHIRE KNIGHT

Little White Lies

Copyright © 2019 by Sapphire Knight

Cover Design by CT Cover Creations

Editing by Mitzi Carroll

Format by Uplifting Author Services

This book is a work of fiction. The names, characters, places, and incidents are products of the writer's imagination or have been used fictitiously and are not to be construed as real. Any resemblance to persons, living or dead, actual events, locales or organizations is entirely coincidental.

All rights reserved. With the exception of quotes used in reviews, this book may not be reproduced or used in whole or in part by any means existing without written permission from the author.

The author acknowledges the trademarked status and trademark owners of various products referenced in this work of fiction, which have been used without permission. The publication/use of these trademarks is not authorized, associated with, or sponsored by the trademark owners.

WARNING

This novel includes graphic language and adult situations. It may be offensive to some readers and includes situations that may be hotspots for certain individuals. This book is intended for ages 16 and older due to some steamy spots. This work is fictional. The story is meant to entertain the reader and may not always be completely accurate. Any reproduction of these works without Author Sapphire Knight's written consent is pirating and will be punished to the fullest extent of the law.

This book is fiction.

The guys are over-the-top alphas.

My men and women are nuts.

This is not real.

Don't steal my shit.

Read for enjoyment.

This is not your momma's cookbook.

Easily offended people should not read this.

Don't be a dick.

Acknowledgements

My husband – I love you more than words can express. Thank you for the support you've shown me. Some days you drive me crazy; other days I just want to kiss your face off. Who knew this would turn out to be our life, but in this journey, I wouldn't want to spend it with anyone else. Thanks for falling for my brand of crazy. I love you, I'm thankful for you, I can't say it enough.

My boys – You are my whole world. I love you both. This never changes, and you better not be reading these books until you're thirty and tell yourself your momma did not write them! I can never express how grateful I am for your support. You are quick to tell me that my career makes you proud, that I make you proud. As far as mom wins go, that one takes the cake. I love you with every beat of my heart, and I will forever.

My Beta Babes – Lindsey K., Patti W., and Wendi H. this wouldn't be possible without you. I can't express my gratitude enough for each of you. Thank you so much!

Editor Mitzi Carroll – Your hard work makes mine stand out, and I'm so grateful! Thank you for pouring tons of hours into my passion and being so wonderful to me. Thank you for your friendship and support.

Cover Designer Clarise Tan – I cannot thank you enough for the wonderful work you've done for me. Your support truly means so much. I can't wait to see our future projects; you always blow me away. You are a creative genius!

Formatting – Thank you so much for making my books always look professional and beautiful. I truly appreciate it and the kindness you've shown me. I know I can depend on you even in short notice and it's so refreshing. You are always quick and efficient, thank you!!!

My Blogger Friends – YOU ARE AMAZING! I LOVE YOU! No, really, I do!!! You take a new chance on me with each book and in return, share my passion with the world. You never truly get enough credit, and I'm forever grateful!

My Readers – I love you. You make my life possible, thank you. I can't wait to meet many of you this year and in the future!

Hil and Vic – Love you two and thank you for always supporting me!

Also By Sapphire

Oath Keepers MC Series
Secrets
Exposed
Relinquish
Forsaken Control
Friction
Princess
Sweet Surrender – free short story
Love and Obey – free short story
Daydream
Baby
Chevelle
Cherry

Russkaya Mafiya Series
Secrets
Corrupted
Corrupted Counterparts – free short story
Unwanted Sacrifices
Undercover Intentions

Dirty Down South Series
1st Time Love
3 Times the Heat
2 Times the Bliss – coming soon

Complete Standalones
Gangster
Unexpected Forfeit
The Main Event – free short story

Oath Keepers MC Collection
Russian Roulette
Tease – Short Story Collection
Oath Keepers MC Hybrid Collection
The Vendetti Duet
Viking - free newsletter short story
Capo Dei Capi Vendetti Duet
The Vendetti Empire - part 1
The Vendetti Queen - part 2

Harvard Academy Elite Duet
Little White Lies
Ugly Dark Truth

Dedicated to:

All of you taking a chance on me for the first time.

Thank you!

Common Terms Cajun French Slang

mon cher – my dear
podnas – partners/friends/brothers
non – no
belle – beauty

Prologue

Tristan

Eleventh grade—again.

Such bullshit to be repeating my junior year, but for Cole, I will. I'll do anything for my brother, even if it means attending an additional year of high school and throwing a wrench in my college plans. It's not that my brother is too stupid to pass the grade; he's just lazy. Hell, I didn't realize the asshole was failing until it was nearly the end of the year and a letter showed up for truancy. We'd gotten them several times in the past, and in response, we'd adapt, randomly missing a class to show up in his place, and my father would step in to make a "donation."

It was too easy since we're identical; at least it was up until high school. Cole is, how should I put it...he's lean. His body is tall and lithe, more like a swimmer's body. He's strong, just not muscular like I am. I plan to play college football, so I hit the weights daily. My brother, however, will major in shamming, I'm sure.

Not only will I be eighteen in eleventh grade, but our father is uprooting us to an entirely different state. Traveling's not the issue; it's giving up the private academy that we've basically run since we hit puberty. The teachers have easily bent to our will, especially being that I'm the best on the football team. They've all loved me. Girls have always been plentiful; even their mothers tend to become giggly around me. Now, however, everything's being shaken up, all because our father has become restless.

Dad's wealthy enough he doesn't need to work, but he enjoys it too much to stop. I guess overthrowing companies *could* be entertaining. Most who cross his path in the business world call him a heartless shark. His company has offices all over the world, so he's home about a week a month. I don't see his reasoning to pack us up and move us practically across the country when he won't be home much anyhow.

We've lived in Louisiana nearly my entire life, and I've loved it there. The South is a different type of living, with our southern belles and wealthy playboys. If you're like me, amongst the richest, then your heart's desire is right at your fingertips, ripe for the plucking. Dear old Dad seems dead set on moving us from the sunshine and warmth to freezing our nuts off in the northeast. We've attempted to "discuss" it, but it's no use. Turning eighteen has lit the fire under our father's ass when it comes to college; he's determined to see his sons into Harvard, Yale, Princeton, Vanderbilt, or Brown University.

Rather than moving us to New York near his office in the city, he's moved us to the middle-of-nowhere Massachusetts. We go from bikinis and suntans to buckets of snow and Harvard Academy—the preparatory school exclusively linked to Harvard University. It takes some serious connections and cash to get in the door, but we're a shoo-in, and faster than I can blink, we're playing footsie with the Northerners. After all, we're the elite.

Chapter One

Kresley

Another day stuck in my miserable life of walking on eggshells around an angry father. He's successful and charming anywhere else, but here, he's just plain mean. He has so many people fooled; they have no clue what it's like to live with him or to be in my shoes. The cutting remarks he randomly makes when he's not happy—for whatever reason—causes my own anger to surface…not that I can act on it, or anything.

I can't help wondering what I ever did to deserve his wrath. Mom may not share in his irritability, but she's still a disappointment to me. She never holds true to anything she says; at least she hasn't in the past. She wants a perfect family and a perfect daughter without doing any actual parenting—though most wealthy people rarely parent their own children. We're usually sent off to boarding schools and raised up by the help. In my case, I'm stuck with Harvard Academy and living each day questioning my life.

I'm not perfect—far from it, in fact, and I'd never fool myself trying to believe otherwise.

I catch grief for burying my head in books and keeping to myself, but in books, I can escape. I can be anywhere and be anyone without someone else criticizing me or causing my anxiety to flair from those invisible eggshells I've tiptoed over for most of my life. It's become routine and I find myself doing it when it's not necessary as well. Running is another tool that I've discovered helps me survive the daily dose of life. No one questions that habit, however. If anything, I'm suddenly invisible—out of sight, out of mind. It also keeps Mom off my back about not being the stereotypical size expected of a rich young lady.

I stumbled into my love of running pretty much by accident. It's not often you meet a teenager who actually enjoys running unless they're on the track team or they're body conscious. I was a bit pudgy growing up—always taller and thicker than the other frail girls in my classes. Mother wasn't amused with having the chubby daughter, though she did her best not to completely wreck my self-image. The summer that I was fourteen years old, dear old, thoughtful Mom sent me away to camp. I guess in her own way, she was protecting my brother and me by getting us out of the house. She claims it was to shoulder the brunt of my father's latest frustrations, even though I'm not sure if I buy it completely. There had to have been something in it for her by sending us away; that's how she's always been.

The camp instructors fully believed in a lot of physical activity amongst not having junk food readily available. Many of us left to go back home leaner, stronger, and most of all, healthier. It was like a fog had been lifted from my mind. I suddenly felt recharged with goals and a future mapped out. Not only that, but I haven't grown an inch since then, and the leaner frame was a blessing in disguise.

For once in my life, my so-called "normal, day to day" didn't feel so acceptable to me anymore. I wanted out of here, and in order to do that, I had to be mentally and physically strong. It's incredible what one summer around the right people can change for a person. I've returned every year since and am not thrilled to be home for the upcoming school year. After an amazing time with people I cherish and respect, I'm thrown back into the fold of chaos, known as my family.

Lady Gaga blares through my headphones as I put one foot in front of the other, my feet pounding away one step at a time on the hot pavement. Her music's so-so, not on my favorites per se, but it's good at helping me zone out. Running and zoning out has fast become my favorite form of self-therapy away from camp.

The cool breeze floats over my flushed skin, perspiration flying off my forehead as I pick up my pace for the last stretch. This is it—my last bit of freedom as tomorrow classes begin again. I'll officially be a junior and one step closer to my plan to get the hell out of my parents' house.

Drawing in a deep breath, I release a controlled, slow exhale as my pace reduces to a power walk. I keep going, rounding in a couple of large circles in the middle of the road in front of our driveway. My body begins to cool down, and my pace slows to measured steps. I can feel eyes on me, and they definitely aren't coming from my own house.

I noticed a few large moving trucks parked two houses over, open to be unloaded. The place is massive, so I can see why they have multiple trucks there. They must be reasonably wealthy to afford it. That's just another thing Father will end up being pissed about, no doubt. He likes to be the top on the neighborhood totem pole, so to speak, and that house is no doubt as big as ours is.

Moving my arm above me, I rest my palm against the rock pillar to the iron fence surrounding our property. Using my free hand, I hike my leg up behind me and begin to stretch out the muscle. With the movement, I catch site of a random guy leaning up against one of the neighboring trees. The shade from the enormous Burr Oak camouflaged him, and I almost didn't notice him. I hadn't even felt his stare as I ran by; it makes me wonder how many others I've passed and hadn't realized it. Not that I care if anyone notices me running or anything. It's just that I should have some sense for my personal safety, even if we are in a quiet, wealthy neighborhood.

With a winded huff, I grab for the water bottle that I'd left next to the gate. Opening wide, I guzzle the refreshment down in large, unladylike gulps. My mother would be chastising me, but I can't bring myself to care in the slightest about that either. I had a good run, and my limbs almost feel like jelly at the moment.

I still sense the guy's eyes in my direction, so I swipe the back of my hand over my mouth and turn to face him. I can only imagine what I must look like. My cropped T-shirt is completely soaked through with sweat, my light lilac-tinted hair is a frazzled mess—even in the ponytail, and my skin's flushed cherry red as if I've been sunburned. I'm definitely not the most attractive I could be, so why on earth has this dude not turned away absolutely repulsed yet? If he's in this neighborhood, he's used to being around pretty, prissy girls if I had to guess, and I'm nothing like that.

"Are you lost?" I ask, waving my hand with a bit more attitude than I'd intended. With closer inspection, I find the guy to be around my own age, with stutter-worthy good looks. Of course, he'd be hot. I'm a wreck at the moment and expect nothing less.

He's practically gawking, and I swear at the rate he's going, his neck may break if he attempts to turn away. In normal circumstances, we'd never be able to speak to our neighbors without calling or emailing. The houses are set so far apart, you can't shout out to your neighbors and be heard. The driveway entrances are somewhat near each other though, as they twist around and meet up with the asphalt, hence me being close enough to ask him now.

He swaggers closer. Yes, I said swagger—there's nothing ordinary with his step. The guy struts as if he owns Country Trails in its entirety. He doesn't though; I know this because my father plays golf with the owner of the housing development that's been built specifically for the upper class. God forbid he has to live around ordinary people or anything. Not that this guy strikes me as ordinary; he's on the opposite end of the spectrum.

"Are you part of the moving crew?" I ask, attempting to get him to speak and break up the awkwardness. It's bad enough that he's so good-looking, I feel like I'm bumbling being the first one to speak.

The Andersons put their mansion on the market, and it sold in three weeks. I was shocked coming home from camp the other day to see the sold sign. I didn't know the couple well, just waved at them occasionally when I was on my runs, and they'd drive past in their bright yellow Bugatti.

"Non." He shakes his head, and I do a double take. His voice is laced with some sort of twang, and my curiosity spikes higher. Does he even speak English? What does *non* mean?

I can't help but wonder if he's on our street looking to rob someone, but I'm familiar with the designer of the shirt he's wearing, and only rich boys can afford a white T-shirt with that twisty logo. They easily sell for seventy-five dollars a pop, and the semi-baggy, dark heather gray sweat pants aren't just your run-of-the-mill department store brand either. My little brother got some just like those a few months back, and my mom dropped two hundred fifteen dollars for them. They're sweats for God's sake, and I happen to know that my sixty-dollar Victoria's Secret yogas are comfier than the more expensive brands. Or maybe I'm wrong, and this guy's been digging through someone else's belongings. It is the night before trash comes to pick up, after all.

"Visiting from the city?" I press on, probing to see if he'll speak another language or if I'd misheard him. I want to know anything about this man currently staring his fill. He's a gorgeous enigma all wrapped up in a white T-shirt and sweat pants. My parents would be absolutely furious if they saw me speaking to him looking like this, and that makes me want to carry on even more.

I meet people from all over the place when I go on my runs. Usually it's one of the neighbor's parents visiting from some foreign country or huge city on their way out for an evening stroll—not a hot guy my age. I'd put him around eighteen or nineteen, a year or two more than my own seventeen years. I know he has to at least be eighteen because his arms, hands, and fingers are covered with colorful ink. Though I guess with enough money you can buy anything, tattoos included. He stands out like a beacon around here with the bad-boy vibe he gives off.

"I'm from the bayou, shorty." With his Southern drawl, his words come out slow with their own twist to the vowels. Shorty sounds more like *shoortaay*, accompanied by his deep, sexy rasp.

"Bayou?" I repeat as my eyebrow hikes and my hand rests on my hip. I can't stop my inquisitiveness and engaging him further in conversation. I should be in the shower at the moment so I have enough time to dress properly before my father returns home.

"Louisiana, beba." It leaves him like *Looosanna, baeba,* and that drawl is hotter than sin.

It must be Cajun French then. I'd heard of it but never met anyone who actually spoke it. And holy-fuck-my-life, that accent is going to be the death of me and every other female in a thirty-mile radius.

"You're a long way from home," I murmur with a soft sigh, needing to fan myself but refraining. Hearing this Cajun boy speak has gotten to me already, my belly quivers with excitement. I want him to talk more. He can say absolutely anything; it doesn't matter, just as long as I can listen to him.

Am I flirting right now? Really?

"S'okay," he shrugs. His eyes are bright with amusement and the dark ink along his shirt collar jumps out with the lazy movement. It's a tease; you can make out the top of a tattoo but not actually see what it is. "Haven't seen a belle as fine as you before, not even out at Blue Bayou with my podnas."

The breeze shifts and I catch the hint of a scent reminding me of Calvin Klein. He smells clean and fresh, far too inviting. Yet everything inside me screams not to be lured in, that he's trouble with a capital T. I don't need any sort of distractions either with school starting up. I made a plan and I'm sticking to it, whether a new guy just so happens to pop up at school or not.

My eyes automatically roll at his unoriginal comment. I'm sure chicks fall all over him for those shortchanged compliments, but I won't be one of them. I don't care how good-looking he is with that sharp, distinctive jawline or the short, sandy-blond hair that's cropped close to the sides of his head and those sparkling cerulean irises. Never mind all the alluring tattoos and the dangerous bad-boy-criminal-street-thug type of vibe he gives off, or how sexy that gravelly Southern drawl is of his.

Jesus, I think with an exhale. I'm in trouble and I've barely said hello. Did I even say hello? I can't remember.

Our stare off is interrupted by another deep voice laced with a similar Southern drawl, only not quite as thick as this delinquent perched in front of me. "Cole?"

The Cajun guy in front of me huffs, not answering the other voice.

"Are you Cole?" I find myself probing, having to know is name. Why's there this ache suddenly panging in my chest as if I need to know, or rather, have to know it? His name will do me no good, only add more fuel to the fire, I'm sure. I should just run along inside and forget that I ever came face-to-face with this hunk of bad boy testing my will to be corrupted.

He nods, his plump lips tilting back up into a cocky smirk that I find far too enticing for my health and well-being. And boy, oh boy, if that smirk doesn't promise mischievous things, I swear! Does he have a girlfriend? Does she know just how naughty this tatted-up male really is? Why am I even going there? It's none of my business! He's not my type, not even remotely close. I shouldn't even be considering him for my type. What has gotten into me?

Glancing over him again, I nod to myself. Yep, he'd definitely be my type if I had one. Shit.

"Cole?" the voice calls again, this time accompanied by a man the same age as him. "Oh, hey." He turns to me with surprise and grins. When he meets my stare, it's like being hit in the face with a pillow. This guy's freaking gorgeous too! And he looks exactly like the other one currently leaning under the tree with a staring problem, minus the peekaboo tattoos and bad-boy vibe. This one, he's like the clean-cut preppy, football player version of the troublemaker that has me salivating.

"Whoa," I say under my breath, catching myself from gaping too noticeably. *I'll add him to my type as well. Shit, what am I saying? I can't go there!*

How on earth are there two guys this good-looking standing right in front of me, right freaking now and I'm covered in sweat and probably a few bugs from my run. "Uh, hi?" I eventually croak out when I'm caught in both of their startling gazes, one gray and the other blue

New guy's grin grows until he's smiling widely. "I see you've met my brother already." He nods his head in Cajun boy's direction. "I'm Tristan." He stands to his full height and I find myself swallowing a bit roughly. He's seriously breathtaking, with his wide chest, strong arms, and longer dark hair. If my best friend, Sam, catches wind of these guys, she'll be camping out on my street in the next blink. Unlike me, she'll take full advantage of these two.

"Brothers?" I repeat a bit breathily, most likely sounding like a baffled idiot. So much for playing it cool in front of the bad boy and now the preppy version. "Are you twins?" I nearly stutter at the near perfect genes in front of me.

Another guy speaks from behind me and I jump, emitting a squeak. "Non." His voice isn't as raspy as Cole and Tristan's but is still laced with a slight twang. "Quads." He walks around me to stand next to Tristan and I find myself openly gaping. I can't stop myself; it's like being hit in the stomach with a bat. I should know, I tried baseball once, it's not for me, trust me on that one.

Holy shit on a stick!

They're damn near the same! He's a bit leaner and has on a

pair of black framed Clark Kent glasses, but you can no doubt see it that they're brothers. Wait, quads? I'm just parting my lips to ask when the fourth and final struts up to join the group. I'm not the only one dripping with sweat...he's shirtless and ripped like he's been working out every single day for the past five years with little sweat droplets cascading down that tight chest and ripped set of abs.

All this perspiration on us and yet my mouth's gone completely dry at the sight of these four.

The latest brother looks me over curiously before turning to his brothers. "You found a stray?" He acts like I'm the new one in the neighborhood, not the other way around.

Tristan hikes his thumb toward Cole. "He did. I just came to get him to stop shammin' and help us unload. Have to give him props, though; we just got here, and he's already found something to like about this place."

"Y-you're unloading all the trucks by yourselves?" Did I just stammer? This is bad, so-so bad. I'm making a fool of myself all because I'm not used to being in the presence and talking to four insanely good-looking people with penises.

Penises. I cringe internally with how fast my mind went south, literally.

The ripped, godlike brother nods and at the same time runs his palm over his stomach before wiping the sweat off onto his jeans. The pants hang deliciously low off his hips; they're light wash denim with the top of his gray boxer briefs peeking out. I could weep, he's so damn perfect. I'm not the type to fawn all over boys my age either, but these four, they're just so much more to look at and then mix in the Southern accent. It's a bit shallow, but I'm a freaking goner, like yesterday.

Tristan takes a step in my direction. "And you are?"

"Me?" I ask, my voice sounding unnaturally breathy at his question. I even point to myself like a dipshit, practically muttering, *you Tarzan, me Jane.* What is it with these four that has my head spinning?

"Yes you," he grins, teasingly. "You have a name, I presume? Or should I call you little lilac?"

Clever, that's my hair color and the fact he's paying close attention to the specific hues even up in a ponytail a sweaty mess, doesn't go unnoticed. "Of course I have a name; I'm the neighbor from over here." I gesture toward the ridiculously opulent entry to our driveway and they all glance over my shoulder. There's a fancy sign with our last name and some iron gates with swirls and such. No one actually needs a gate like that, but Dad thought it "made a statement"—whatever that's supposed to mean.

"Well, nice to meet you neighbor girl, but we have stuff to do." The ripped one grumbles, gesturing for his brothers to follow. I wonder if he's the oldest and plays up the bossy, older brother role.

Cole flicks his sparkling azure gaze over me one last time. The move is leisurely, a bit more of a touchless caress against my flesh. He reminds me of a lazy cat, a panther maybe, but still a cat regardless.

Tristan beams a bright white, charming smile. "I'm sure we'll see you around." He winks before turning away to follow abs and Cajun boy.

The last brother just shrugs, shooting me a small shy grin and follows the other three back toward the massive house across the street. He's got a comic book rolled up and tucked into his back pocket that looks as if it may fall out at any moment. He seems kind of nerdy, but even with the glasses, he's still as hot as the others.

Cajun boy, the jock, Clark Kent and abs—those four guys are going to turn this town completely upside down in a matter of minutes, I can tell already. With them retreating, my heart finally begins to slow to its normal pace and I can breathe regularly once again. Could they be the moving crew for the new family that bought the house? I know one thing that's for certain: they don't make guys like that around here. If they did, everyone within a hundred miles would know who they are.

My phone beeps, further pulling me from their spell and I hightail it down the driveway, back to my shell of a home and normal, boring life.

Chapter Two

Pulling into my usual parking space at Harvard Academy, I put my car in park. It's toward the back of the lot, but I don't mind. I've learned it's easier to leave after my last class being parked out here rather than right up front. I claimed the parking spot next to my best friends when we both got our licenses last year. She rolls in, parking her dark blue BMW in her space as soon as my Jag's in her rightful spot.

We're a lot alike, but also very different. We're both book nerds and work hard to get good grades, but that's where the similarities end. I'm reserved; she's outgoing. My home life is a wreck; hers is picture perfect. Not that I fault her for it, more like the opposite. I have lilac hair hitting midback while she has ebony locks brushing her waist. I keep my nose in my own business while she's so nosey; she's even on the school paper.

I wouldn't say we're necessarily popular. We're friends with practically everyone, but I'm also not the first one being invited to parties. More like we get a last-minute text and I never go. I know Sam wants to, but she can never talk me into it. I'd rather study, so I can earn a full scholarship to college and get as far away from my parents fakeness as possible.

Grabbing my bag, I slam the door behind me as I climb out to greet my friend. "Hey, Sam."

"Hey, girl." She smiles, rounding the car and I get my first glimpse at her outfit. She's in a schoolgirl outfit; white button up shirt, tied high enough to show off her belly button. Her skirt's short enough that there's no way she can bend over.

"Dude," I say with a giggle, taking her in. "You look hot, but I feel like someone's going to tell you to give Brittany Spears her outfit back."

She scoffs. "Your first thought was hot, so it's the only one that counts. And never mind that we know who that I;, we'll pretend that we never went through that phase in fifth grade." She cringes and I laugh again.

"I look like a nun compared to you." Shaking my head, I glance at my outfit again. I chose a yellow sundress with Kate Spade wedges to start off the school year. It took every ounce of courage for me to wear it in front of my peers. No matter how in shape I get, I still feel like people stare at me. I thought my dress would stand out, with it stopping a few inches above my knees and the formfitting material around my generous-sized chest, but not with Samantha's getup. The academy allows us to wear whatever we want on the first and last day of school; otherwise, we all have the same boring uniform to wear every day.

The parking lot vibrates under my feet, everyone's heads turning toward the booming sound. "Sail" by Machine Gun Kelly blares piercingly, speakers so loud the bass vibrates everything in the immediate area. A matte black Aston Martin Vanquish with matching rims whips into the parking lot, and if it weren't for it being a convertible, I doubt it'd have any windows left. My mouth gapes open like a fish as I watch, shocked. The music shuts off and four *big* boys hop out of the tiny sports car. I'm surprised their large frames fit. My brother has a Maserati, which is close in size and even I hate sitting in the back seat.

No way in hell. I swallow, staring like everyone else as it clicks in my mind as to who just showed up at my school. I can't believe they're here right now. It certainly makes me wish I'd spoken to them more so I could've had a heads-up that they'd be attending here when school started back up.

With matching black backpacks in hand, they head for campus as one powerful mass. Random students yell compliments on either the car or the music as they pass by and the quarterback of the football team practically runs over to greet the new guys. Of course, it was Cole driving; with music like that, I'd expect nothing less. But holy cow balls, they're here at my school! I thought they were too old to be in school here and that means...well, they weren't the movers at all. They're my new neighbors—all four of them—and I'm an idiot to not grasp that sooner.

With a groan at the realization, my hand flutters up to cover my mouth. I hope they don't tell anyone about running into me. Not that I care much about what people think of me; I don't want it to embarrass Sam. Unlike me, she actually cares about all that stuff—like popularity and what guys think of her.

Tristan casts a quick look in my direction before they head inside. He pauses long enough to send me a wink and my jaw drops again. Twice in a matter of minutes I've been thrown off my game and the year has merely just begun. This can't be a good sign. A hand hits my stomach, garnering my attention. I glance over to find Sam staring at me, one eyebrow hiked.

Shit.

"I totally saw that. Do you know those guys?"

Swallowing down my voice, I head for the school, wanting to get my stuff in my locker and to my new class in time to get a good seat. And maybe I don't want Sam to have a good view of my face when I thwart her question. "I was at camp all summer, remember?" It's my excuse for everything each year, and so far, it's worked like a charm.

"Well yeah, but the dark-haired hottie in the Vanquish just

winked. Everyone witnessed that it was at you and not me. Unless you think he had something in his eye? It looked like a wink to me, though." She's not being unkind about it; I know Sam would never be ugly like that over a guy. Besides, I can't believe he would actually wink at me, especially here, in front of people.

"Out of everyone here, I doubt they'd pay attention to me." I brush the comment off as her car lock chirps right before we get into the main hall. It's wide and lined with pristine lockers. Students are peppered around, talking excitedly about their summers. Smiling, I offer Sam a thumbs-up at the double car chirp, hoping to distract her. She always forgets to lock her beamer and I'm surprised she remembered today. If it were me, my father would skin me alive, but that's neither here nor there.

"They? As in plural? You do know them?" She stays right on track, nosier than ever.

Turning to face her when we get to my locker, I key in my code. I know the number by heart and can enter it without looking; I've kept the same number since freshman year. The locker quietly clicks open. It's a small perk of attending a private academy full of rich kids; we get buttons rather than a combination or a key. "I swear it, I don't know them. But, I may have seen them when I was on my run yesterday." It's technically not a lie.

"No way!" Her eyes light up and I turn away, tossing my bag into my locker. I take my cell, pencil pouch, and a small binder out to keep with me. It's the first day back, so I don't expect much work, and besides, we use laptops or tablets most the time anyhow. We'll probably just go over syllabuses, expectations, class rules, and more of the same boring first day pep talks. "I hope I have them in at least one of my classes," she gushes excitedly, giving me a small, eager shake. "They'd definitely make math interesting for me, that's for sure."

Rolling my eyes as I close the metal door and hold the lock button, I refrain from admitting that I'd secretly enjoy having one of them in math as well. Although, I'm sure we'd learn nothing if they did happen to show up to one of our classes. "I want a good seat so I'm headed to AP English. I'll see you for third," I mumble and trail off toward class. She throws me a hasty wave and jets hurriedly in the opposite direction.

That math class she spoke of just so happens to be third period, which is the class we have together, and the last thing I need is one of those four in there with us. Sam would not leave me alone if they were. Hell, no female in the class would be able to function properly around them. I don't think I have anything to worry about when it comes to shared class schedules though. They strike me as seniors just floating through their last year. They're probably concentrating on doing as many females as possible and the bare minimum on actual work. I've learned over the years that seems to be the main agenda for senior guys—other than graduating.

"'Sup, Kres?" I'm pulled into a strong embrace and lifted off my feet by an oversized warm body as I enter the class.

"Brandon Tompkins, put the young lady down," the teacher chides, adjusting her glasses as she witnesses our exchange. I beam a bright smile at Brandon and pat his arm until he finally sets me on my feet and gives me some breathing room.

"Hi, Brandon," I greet with an amused grin and turn to apologize. "Sorry about that, Mrs. Lawkins."

"Just take a seat you two, and preferably, two separate seats. I've already been warned that Brandon is known for sitting on your desk during classes."

Cringing a little, I shoot her an apologetic smile. Brandon will no doubt keep our instructor on her toes. He's a handful, but by the end of the year he's usually most of the teachers' favorite student, especially the women.

He hoots, making a loud mess of the situation. "What! You've been gossiping in the teachers' lounge, Mrs. Lawkins? Or, do you mind if I call you Sandra? I think I like the way Sandra sounds better; you seem younger." He flirts and she rolls her eyes again. He's a good friend of mine, but unlike him, I prefer not to have the instructors attention directed toward me.

"Mr. Tompkins, take your seat, please."

"Oh and a dominatrix as well," he mutters on the way to a desk, making the class choke out the snickers they'd been attempting to hold back.

He squeezes my bicep lightly and sits in the chair to my right. I've been friends with Brandon since kindergarten. He's wanted to date me for a while now, but I just can't think of him that way. I like him too much as a friend. I've heard that his gaggle of followers is upset, too, because they all want him, but he won't date them. Supposedly, he's holding out until I see the light. Unfortunately for him, it'll never happen. I've told him that very thing before, too, but he still holds off on committing to anyone. I know he randomly dates; I've had a few people ask if it bothered me, but I always assure them that it doesn't. I want him to find a girl that he likes and she feels the same way for him in return.

It's not that I don't find him attractive either, because I'm pretty sure every female in the entire school does. Brandon's got that whole sweet, outgoing, dimples vibe about him. He's super tall, around six foot five or something, too, so he basically smothers you if he decides to hug you. If he does, there's no squirming away either. I think his muscles have muscles from playing so much football and baseball. It's hard to resist his charm when paired with his big brown eyes resembling melted chocolate. Despite all of that, I see him like a brother—not that it deters him from attempting to change my mind on the matter.

The class instantly becomes silent, drawing my attention away from Brandon. My gaze tiredly trails over each of my classmates before finally coming to stop at the front of the room. The cause for the sudden quiet and curious stares is none other than one of the new guys.

I should've known right away too. And how did I get stuck with one of them first thing in the morning? This is AP; none of my new neighbors struck me as English buffs. But then again,

I'd thought they were the moving guys. I had no idea they were a group of spoiled rich boys and I'd practically stuck my foot in my mouth when I met them all. Then they'd made such a commotion pulling into the parking lot this morning that I've basically remained in a state of frazzled nerves since first interacting with the four of them. This is so bad. I don't have room for distractions this year or next.

He locks his gaze with mine and it's far too alluring to turn away. I shouldn't stare—people are going to start talking if I do, and I don't want to be anyone's next topic of gossip. Rumors spread like wildfire here and I'm doing everything I can to keep a low profile and get the hell out with a scholarship.

His gray orbs remain on me with each step he takes down the aisle. One foot after the other, he draws nearer, and it's as if I'm in a trance, unable to look away. After an awkward moment of us staring at each other, he takes the seat directly to my left, looking toward the front. I could reach out and touch him if I wanted, but I don't do it. We're not friends; we don't even know each other.

He turns to me, catching my lingering stare on his profile. Pulling the glasses free from his collar, he places the obsidian framed specs on and offers me a shy smile. It's him, the geekier one of the bunch. It's not fair for me to call him that because there is absolutely nothing geeky about him. Oh no, he's one hundred percent gorgeous just like his brothers. His irises are ash, though, not cobalt like Cole's. I tuck that small detail away for later if I'm faced with them all at once like before. I don't remember if the four of them all have different colored irises. I'll have to try and get a good look sometime.

"Hi again," he murmurs quietly, being friendly. My mouth goes dry at the smooth, deep timbre. I had forgotten how low their voices were when we'd spoken before or how they all have that Southern twang mixed in with their words. Cole's accent was much more pronounced, but I can definitely hear the easy drawl in Clark Kent's words.

"Hi," I reply with a friendly smile. I don't want him to think I'm some weirdo who only sweats and stares at people like I had after my run. They caught me at a very unflattering time of the day.

"I, uh, didn't catch your name yesterday." His Adams apple bobs as he tugs at his black collared shirt a little, as if it's constricting around his throat. It's not, but maybe he's shy after all? I can't imagine him not having girlfriends that are prettier than me though. The guy is just that hot. Hell, they all were—sexy, like you see on TV.

"I'm Kresley," I whisper, attempting to not draw additional attention to us. "Most people around here call me Kres though." I shrug, not wanting to admit that not many people call me anything because only a few speak to me on a daily basis.

"I'm Axel," he supplies and my stomach pitter-patters with excitement and anxiety all rolled into one. It's been too long since this school had a new student, and now we have four of them—all on the same day. I'm sure my stomach isn't the only one doing flips at seeing these guys. There's no doubt in my mind that every girl in school has their sights set on the quads already.

"I remember you," I admit and his smile grows. His teeth are perfect. Pearly white and straight, and now I can't stop myself from imagining what it'd be like to kiss him. Not that he'd ever kiss me or anything, but I can't stop thinking of his mouth.

His irises aren't just any old gray either. They remind me of a rainy day when the clouds are a darker shade from the stormy weather. His hair is short and styled neatly, his nose narrow and strong, but not too big for his face. And his lips...they're the impeccable bit of plumpness that you just know when he kisses you that you'll get lost in him. He's the type of boy I could sit and stare at all day long discovering each and every little thing that makes him uniquely him.

So it turns out that maybe I am a sweater and starer. Jesus. I'm going to embarrass myself with them by the end of the year. I can feel it.

"You look beautiful today."

I swallow, taking his compliment in and open my mouth to respond when my hair is tugged from the opposite direction. I turn, finding Brandon. He's got my hair twisted around his finger and a territorial glare pointed at Axel.

"Are you okay?" I whisper at my angry friend.

"The teacher was speaking to you, but you were in la—la land. Pay attention up front."

I want to huff and roll my eyes but hold myself back. He's only trying to make sure I don't get detention on the first day back. I can't fault him for looking out, especially because I know that if I get detention, he'll do something to end up with the punishment as well. While it may not be a big deal for me to stay after school and do my homework, Brandon's coach would be furious at him for being late to football practice and I don't want him getting in trouble on my account.

Nodding, I sit back in my chair and pay attention. That's how I stay for the remainder of class, too, because I know if I move or look to my left, that I won't be able to turn away from Axel. He's far too enticing, especially knowing that he's smart enough for this class. He's obviously not all good looks and muscles. Did I mention he has muscles too? Not the big *in your face* kind like Brandon's or Axel's brother's abs and jock boy, but you can definitely see that he'd pack a punch if he were to throw one. I imagine you'd have to be able to hold your own growing up with three brothers.

One thing's for certain, I'm going to have my hands full when Sam gets a good look at the four of them. And if the thought of her having crushes on them upsets me, then I can only imagine how it'll be seeing them with a new girl on their arm each week. This is going to be a long year and it's only begun.

Chapter Three

"I know who they are," Sam bursts, full of energy as soon as I see her at lunch the following day. The servers walk around each of the filled tables asking if we want anything from their trays. I opt for the grilled lemon chicken and Sam grabs a filet mignon and Waldorf salad.

"Oh?" I comment as our food's placed in front of us and Brandon makes his way toward our table from the jocks. Surprisingly, I didn't see Tristan amongst their fold, but I imagine it won't be long before I do. I'm not startled at Sam's declaration; I figured she'd be all over it. Not that I really want to discuss guys in front of Brandon, however. We're only friends, sure, but it has to be uncomfortable for him when I know he's wanted to date me in the past.

Her grin blossoms and I can tell she's on the verge of squealing in excitement. "French aristocrats!"

"They're too young...or something." I wave her guess off.

She snorts. "Not the guys, silly, their ancestors. They come from old money and holy shit they are superduper wealthy. You know that billionaire that just pledged one hundred million euros to help rebuild the Notre Dame Cathedral?"

Wincing, I think of that beautiful structure and the devastation. "Of course, the fire is a tragedy. I hope they catch the terrorists that started it. We all know it was arson even if the media likes to hide the truth from the world."

Brandon pulls out the vacant chair beside me and sits, leaning over with his arm resting on the back of my chair. We always sit like this though. He hangs with his football buddies until Sam and I get our food and then he makes his way over to sit with us. It's not every day, but it happens enough that Sam doesn't even blink when he leans in to listen. He's nosey like she is.

She continues, ignoring the interruption. "That guy is their grandfather, the billionaire."

My mouth drops open a little. "How do you know all this?" I ask, as Brandon turns to stare at me. His attention doesn't go unnoticed, but I play it off like I'm not paying any attention.

"I Googled, as has half the school." Her eyes widen, like I'm dense for asking. "The other half knows from those of us too impatient to wait," she fills in and I snort.

"Of course they do," I murmur, not missing the exasperated look she shoots my way before pasting another big smile on her mouth. I cut into my chicken, lifting my fork and Brandon dives in to steal the bite.

"Hey!" A giggle breaks free and I grin his way. "I was going to eat that."

He shrugs. "I know, but I was tired of hearing about the new guys. Everyone has been talking about them and I'm over it."

"Have you seen them?" Sam interrupts. "Of course, we're all taking about them; they're hot and rich...oh, and in case you missed it, they're hot and rich!" she repeats and Brandon scoffs in return.

A shadow falls over our table; it takes me a second to realize that the lunchroom has grown suspiciously quiet. Glancing up, my mouth pops open. It seems to be a bad habit when I'm around these guys. Cole's glaring menacingly at Brandon and I quickly flash a look beside me to see he's returning the look right back at the Cajun.

"Uh, hi?" I manage to squeak and Axel greets quietly, "Hey, Kres."

Tristan's mouth turns up into a cocky smirk. "May we join you?"

"Me?" I ask as Sam snorts beside me. A growl comes from the big brute on my other side as Cole's startling sapphire gaze finds mine.

"Mon cher," Cole murmurs.

Brandon grumbles, "Like hell," and I smack his firm thigh.

"Abs" folds his arms across his wide, muscular chest, filling up the space even more, if that's possible. Brandon is a big dude, but this guy's a tank all on his own as well, let alone throw in three brothers to his side. They're certainly their own force.

Sam breaks through my awkward pause with a bright, welcoming smile. "Of course! Please join us. I'm Samantha Collingsworth by the way."

Cole snorts, muttering something under his breath as they pull the chairs out and take the vacant seats. Tristan meets my gaze. "Would you like to introduce us?" he asks, being the gentleman and I silently chide myself for being the muted idiot. I'm so damn rude and that's not my usual MO.

Drawing in a breath, I attempt not to stutter when Brandon tucks a loose strand of hair behind my ear. I swear he got closer in the last few seconds, and it wouldn't surprise me if he scoots me on his lap. It's not out of the ordinary for him to do it and I've let the actions—his polite possessiveness—go on for far too long. "Guys, this is my best friend, Sam, and I've been friends with Brandon since I was five." I don't know why I share that bit about knowing Brandon for so long, maybe so the quads have a small understanding of our closeness. Brandon is not my boyfriend, by any means, but I won't put him on the spot coming out and saying that at the moment.

Clearing my throat, I gesture to the group in front of me. "Meet my new neighbors…Axel." I nod toward Clark Kent. Gesturing at Cole next, I continue, "Cajun, the jock, and abs." I use their nicknames as I have to draw a line somewhere. They can't realize they've frazzled me so much already, and Sam would easily catch on to my little fib from before when I said I didn't know them. It wasn't technically a lie and I don't know why I felt the need to hold back in the first place, but it's too late now to change my previous decision.

The guys stare at me, fully amused by my nicknames I've assigned to them. The jock speaks first with a chuckle. "I'm Tristan, but thanks for the jock compliment. I did help my team take home a trophy last year and was voted most valuable player." He shrugs, clearly not shy about letting the world know he's talented.

Brandon's body stills, his muscles flexing. "Shame you had to leave then, as that's *my* title here."

Tristan flicks his intense stare to the man next to me, acting as if it's the first time he's noticed the massive form hovering over me like a possessive boyfriend. "Shame indeed. Let's hope we don't play the same position," he throws out and it's like lines being drawn in the sand. "I keep my spot no matter where I play.

Cole chuckles. "Cajun, hmm, beba?" His icy glare cuts from Brandon to soften on me as he says it.

"It was that or tattoos," I admit reluctantly and he chuckles again, amused.

"Mon cher, I'm Cole. Thought you'd remember it though, as you were sweaty and panting at the time." He flashes a devilish grin that has my heart stammering in my chest. His words sound naughty even though I know he's referring to catching me after my run. No one else around here knows that minor detail though.

Brandon's chair scrapes, loudly echoing and goes flinging backwards as he stands and nearly roars in anger. The four across from me jump to their feet, chests puffed, ready for a fight. It's enough to garner the attention of the entire room, much to my mortification. I hate being the center of attention and this throw-down that's about to take place no doubt has me right smack dab in the center. This is not my scene. I'm quiet and kind and keep to myself.

Abs growls low in his throat, the sound rumbling through his chest. His quiet dominance rearing its head once again, as he warns, "Be really careful with what you do next. I'll paint this table with your face."

I nearly choke at the raspy threat and Sam gasps beside me. Quickly hopping up, eager to defuse this building tension, I clutch Brandon's rigid bicep. "Go for a run, Brandon. Please," I plead, not wanting these four to hurt him. He's my friend and I want to protect him however I can, even if it's merely getting him to leave. I have no doubt in my mind that my new neighbors can hold their own, no matter how big the other guy is. "You have a game coming up and you know how much the team needs you." It's the only thing I can think of to get him distracted. The team is everything to him...well, besides me. I gaze up at him, wanting him to see how much I need him to listen to me. Brandon usually does his own thing and others seem to roll with it, but he needs to take my advice on this.

His pissed off coffee-colored irises meet mine before he rips his thick arm free and storms off. I've never seen him act like that before and find my hands a bit shaky as I meet the stares of the brothers in front of me and take my seat once again. Drama has never been my thing and I have no idea what to say or do at the moment to break up what just happened. It escalated so quickly that I almost want to believe it hadn't happened at all. Everyone's curious stares quickly push the wishful thinking away. They'll no doubt be whispering about it for the remainder of the day.

Sam sighs again. "Wow...so that was kinda hot," she admits

and I hush her. It works to break up the tension, though, as the guys flash smug grins and sit back down like it's an everyday occurrence to them. For all I know, it could be. Our school is going to love every minute of it too. Whatever—I can't be caught up in the whirlwind of drama; it's not in my plan.

"Why does Ax get called by his name and we don't?" Abs grumbles after a beat. While he seems moody, it's cute to witness him pout about such a trivial detail.

"He has a nickname too," I admit with a shrug. "It's just that... well, he's been sweet to me." Besides, I don't want to single him out with his different name. Who knows if it'll offend him and that's the last thing I want to do. He seems to be the calmest of the four, so I highly doubt he'd speak up about it. Regardless, I don't want to put him on the spot.

Axel's brows shoot up. "Really? What's mine?" He's eager and that can be good or bad. He probably won't even get it, but who knows. He did have that comic book rolled up in his jeans pocket.

My cheeks burn. I know they're turning red; I can feel the heat. I'm embarrassed, even though I'm the one to call them by nicknames in the first place. I don't want to hurt his feelings. I was serious about him being sweet so far. I don't want him to think that he doesn't measure up to his brothers' names, because he most certainly does. With a groan, I stare down at my plate of now cold chicken and manage to whisper, "Clark Kent."

There's a whistle from one of them, drawing my attention back to Axel. He looks shocked before finally smiling broadly at his brothers and professing, "Never had a girl call me Superman before."

Blowing out a heavy breath, I smile his way again. I never thought of Clark Kent turning into Superman, but if he takes his glasses off along with his shirt...well, it could happen. Not that he needs to. I like his glasses just fine. He looks smart and that's just as sexy as his brothers having abs.

"Abs," Tristan smirks, holding back a laugh and gestures to his ripped brother, "is actually our broody brother, Brent."

My gaze locks with Brent's intense stare and I swallow back my humiliation at his subjective nickname. He certainly doesn't seem fazed in the slightest at hearing it. He probably gets it a lot but I don't want to be one of those girls. His tongue darts out to lick his full bottom lip that's so much like Ax's, my eyes eagerly following the move. I could stare at him all day and that's a distraction I definitely don't need. One way to pin him down besides his muscles is the slight crook in his nose. The other guys' noses are perfectly straight, but Brent's looks like it may have been broken at some point. There's even a tiny, light scar running across the bridge. Hard to believe, but the scar makes him even sexier in my opinion, not that he needs help in the attractive department.

"Are you the oldest?" I blurt and his head tilts, his calculating gaze moving from casual to finally really taking me in. It's like he doesn't pay much attention to anything, as if he's distracted. He and Cole definitely have the 'whatever' attitude in common.

"I am." His voice is a gravely rasp. Jesus, if I were the praying type, I'd be making the sign of the cross. He has that low tone, the type you feel right down to your core.

At first guess, you'd think he never talks, but after his threat earlier, maybe it's the opposite and he shouts at his brothers. Whatever his story is, I'm beyond interested in finding it out. Cole strikes me as the family bad boy at first glance, but I have a feeling I couldn't be more wrong and this is the dangerous brother. Easily overlooked beside his brothers' outgoing personalities, aside for his bulk, he reminds me of something...but what? My gaze widens as I watch him pull out a preportioned container of chicken breast and brown rice. No one brings lunch from home. The schools chefs are spectacular but I doubt Brent gives two thoughts to what anyone else thinks.

"They have that here." I nod at his Tupperware then gesture to my own plate. It's full of nearly identical food.

"They don't weigh their portions," he mumbles before digging into his cold food. I only know what he means because of my conditioning camp I attend each summer. They weigh everything when it comes to meals and they teach us to do the same. I don't keep it up when I'm home, but I have a general idea of how much to place on my plate. Brent's the first person I've come across to speak about food like that to me outside of camp, and it's refreshing to find a kindred food spirit and know I'm not alone with it here.

Sam nudges me and I jump a bit. "Guys, this is my best friend, Sam," I blurt in a rush and she giggles.

"You already said that."

"Oh." I find myself turning red all over again. A nervous laugh breaks free from my mouth when I catch her beaming at me. She's thoroughly amused. I'll be hearing about this for forever, no doubt.

"You've certainly made an impression on our Kresley," she fills in as I grow quiet. "Hell, even on the entire school," she declares and the guys nod, looking like it's to be expected.

"We're used to it," Ax admits with an easy shrug. His nonchalant comment has my mind racing. Sam didn't have time to share much of anything else with me about the quads' family, but I wonder if they move around a lot as well and are used to this type of treatment. That has to suck if it's the case.

Tristan picks up from his brother's comment, carrying on. "We were kind of popular at our last school," he divulges and Cole rolls his eyes.

"What he means is we ran that fucking school and we'll do the same here." Cole shoots me an arrogant smirk as he stands and sends a chin-lift to his brothers. "I'm out."

Brent trains his broody glare on his fleeing brother. "It's the first day and you're already ditching? Seriously, man?"

Cole just shrugs and saunters off without a care in the world it'd appear.

"Is everything okay?" I find myself inquisitively asking. I should keep my mouth closed as it's none of my business. Nothing about them is of any concern to me. I'm friendly but that doesn't mean I need any new friends in my life, especially the complicated sort and they scream 'high maintenance.'

Brent doesn't respond with anything, but Tristan speaks up, "He's fine, Kresley. Thanks for checking. Our brother takes a lot of half days. You'll see him coming and going; it's just the way he is."

"Is that why you guys look older? Did he fail a grade or something?" What is wrong with me today? It's Sam's thing to ask all the probing questions, not mine. I can't seem to stop myself from spilling them as they come to me though. My normal filter seems to be broken with these four.

Axel mutters, "He's smart. He just doesn't like showing up. It wasn't a big deal until he got the tattoos. It's not like I can just remove my glasses and easily pretend to be him anymore."

My gaze widens. It finally hits me as to why they all look older and not just Cole. They're quadruplets—closer than other siblings—and I'm an idiot not to get it right away. I never would have guessed if it weren't for them being in some of my classes as well. "Oh my God, you *all* stayed back a grade to be with him, didn't you?" That's dedication, not allowing your sibling to be left behind, even if it entails an extra year of high school.

Brent casts an irritated glance at Sam before looking at me once more; clearly he doesn't like people knowing his business. I can understand that, as the rich are quick to judge if you don't put on the illusion of being perfect. "There's nothing more important than family, than having each other's backs."

With a tight nod, I swallow. They did fail a grade to be with their brother. Their loyalty is on an entirely different level than most. The lunch bell chimes, saving me from making his statement awkward in a way I seem to easily do when it comes to this group.

Before I can make a quick exit, Axel comes to my side. "Come on, Lois Lane. I'll walk you to next period."

It takes me nearly all day before his comment registers and I realize that he gave me my own nickname too. He didn't call me something random either, but rather, the one woman Superman could never get enough of. He fell hard for Lois and saved her many times. If I thought my heart was beating fast before, it has nothing on the butterflies now filling my tummy at Axel's thoughtfulness. Anyone can be good-looking, but intelligence and wit mixed in is a dangerous combination—dangerous to my heart.

Chapter Four

*S*itting quietly, I tap my sty's plush tip against the lab table. I can't help but watch the door as Tristan strolls into biology class with a different girl tucked under each of his muscular arms. He's so handsome it makes my stomach flip whenever I'm anywhere remotely close to him—orany of the brothers, for that matter. His silky dark locks glint under the bright florescent lights, looking almost as if there's a bluish tint to the hue. With his charcoal irises, it's almost painful to gaze at him up close, but no one can help it. Everyone stares. I mean…everyone. Even the staff. He's beautiful; they all are.

The boys have been in school for three days and are already at the top of the school's proverbial food chain. I'm beginning to believe that even the elite of Harvard Academy—the richest enrolled in school—want to either date any of them or actually be them. Pretty soon the guys will take over the elite title, too, as their assets surpass anyone's here. It's a twisted case of hero worship and the worst part is that I can't even fault them for it. The guys have done nothing whatsoever for me to have a negative thought in my mind toward them. I've never commended even an ounce of the attention that they seem to garner no matter where they are. I can't imagine the amount of pressure they must constantly face. I'd be exhausted, yet they don't appear fazed in the least. In fact, Tristan's so charming and charismatic, you'd think he was created to be in the spotlight.

Am I jealous? *Of course not.*

A prominent social status in our ridiculously privileged private school is not one of my life goals and it never has been. My father cares about being at the top of the hierarchy at his business, but that's not my personal cup of tea. Now, am I envious of the girls I always see holding on to Tristan in the hallways, at the boys' car, the lunch room or in classes? That would be a yes, even if I don't want to come to terms with my emotions when it involves the quads. It's natural to crave the feeling of being wanted, especially by the best-looking guys in school. I'll get over it eventually, once their novelty wears off, I'm sure.

Each of the girls peppers a kiss on Tristan's cheeks and I try not to show a reaction so blatantly obvious on my face having witnessed them touch him like that. Silently I groan as our teacher gestures toward me sitting right up front. He draws everyone's attention in my direction and I wish I could shrink into my seat, but I know that won't help. "Tristan, since you've arrived late, you get to partner with Kresley. She's gotten the best grades out of the entire academy the past two years and I have a feeling you may be requiring the extra help as we get into our lessons." My face burns with the instructor's underhanded praise and I tuck my chin lower to escape from the stares.

They may not be from around here, but the instructor is acting as if Tristan didn't just come from a top-notch school. He must be smart to have decent enough grades to allow him to play sports. Though it wouldn't really surprise me much to discover if past professors have helped him out by tweaking his grades to keep him playing. I'm not saying he's ever used that to his advantage, but when you're surrounded by the filthy rich, you learn that nearly everything can be bought, especially a measly grade or attendance into a top-notch college.

Tristan handles the dig good-naturedly, plopping onto the seat next to me at the shared lab table. We'd all been sitting in different spots the past few days since school started, but that all changed today due to the level of talking going on. Now we're all stuck in new places, sitting quietly, and of course, the class's attention is focused solely on Tristan, and by default, me.

His large, well-built frame takes up more space than the average person and I find myself suddenly feeling warmer than a moment before. His presence being this close to mine has my heart beating so fast I'd almost believe he could hear the thump-thump if it wasn't physically impossible. Although if my pulse was checked right now, I'd no doubt be asked to lie down and give it a rest. It's like running a mile while zombies chase behind, only Tristan is far from them when it comes to his Southern allure and enticingly good looks.

He sends me a grin followed by a wink and I swallow tightly to keep my expression neutral. These guys have way too much influence over me already. Tristan leans in, his warm breath grazing my ear as he confesses in a whisper, "Exactly the seat I wanted anyway." His fresh man smell envelops me with his nearness and I find myself inhaling deeply like a giant weirdo.

I don't say anything; I can't, because I'm too dumbstruck to reply. It'll come out in an embarrassing squeak or croak or who knows what. I've been around these brothers for a total of four days. How on earth can I already be crushing so desperately on them? And it's not just one guy that has mine and everyone else's attention; it's all four of them.

Cole wasn't kidding when he said they'd run the school. The year has merely begun, and it seems that they've already taken over. I can only imagine what a little more time will offer them.

Rather than attempt to utter a generic reply, I tap the computer that's in the surface of the lab desk. It's a smooth, dark top that lights up with your applied body heat. All you have to do is press your finger or hand down for five seconds in the center and it brings the system to life for the course. Each day we log on and do our class work on it together in pairs. We're each individually issued tablets with our lockers as well to take home and use to complete independent homework. I'd rather use my laptop for everything, but supposedly this system helps the school keep cheating to a minimum.

"Axel has a desk like this too," Tristan randomly shares and my gaze widens.

"A, um, biology desk?" I mutter stupidly and he chuckles, his voice rich and raspy and delicious like a gooey chocolate donut. I may've skipped breakfast again, but with my mother on my heels I have to most days.

"No *sugar plum*, a desk with the screen built in to the surface. He's always writing down formulas or drawing his next masterpiece. He's more talented than the three of us put together."

"He's an artist?" My head tilts as I get lost in his steel gaze. His eyes are intense—the kind that once you look, you can't seem to turn away. Not that I'd want to or anything. They remind me of deep water during a storm, the dark, murky gray with an occasional lighter splash mixed in. He's devastatingly handsome, and in this moment, I know one thing for certain: Tristan could easily ruin me for anyone else if he wanted. In fact, if his brothers are anything like he is, I bet they all could and that has warning signals firing all over the place in my mind.

His mouth kicks up into another perfect white grin. "How about you come over tonight and I'll show you? I'll show you a few other things too."

I'm naïve, but not that gullible to fall for his suggestion. He's been surrounded by different girls every time I see him and I'm not about to spend any time alone with him, especially at his house. "I'm good, but thanks," I reply and his mouth drops open, stunned at my rebuff. Obviously, he's used to getting what he wants but I have some sense of self-preservation. I have a plan in full effect and I'm not about to let him shake that up any more than their presence alone has managed to do.

"You're joking," he states, clearly not used to being turned down by the female population. "Tomorrow then," Tristan affirms and I shake my head at that also. It's a no from me on any day.

"Not then either." I eventually lower my eyes to the desk, glancing over the assignment. We have to read the paragraphs and take any notes we may need for the upcoming project. At least with Tristan as my partner I'll be able to do all the work and secure a good grade. I usually despise group projects, thinking my grades would be better if I could do them on my own. At least there's some advantage to having the flirt sitting beside me.

"Mm, mm..." I can hear the smile coating his voice as he leans in close again. With an almost mocking tone, he whispers a little too close for my comfort. "You're a tease. Aren't you, my darling? It's all right. I happen to enjoy a good challenge." His breath flutters over my ear with his words, and I draw in a quick breath. I'm not used to guys like him or his brothers. Other than Brandon, most of the males in school keep their distance. I'd thought maybe I wasn't very pretty or I was too quiet, that they never paid any real attention my way. That doesn't seem to be the case where Tristan is concerned and I have a feeling this is going to be a long year in biology if he doesn't give up his newfound challenge of getting into my pants.

"Why are we going this way?" I ask Sam as she carts me out through the back doors of the academy toward the vast sports fields. School's finished for the day and I'm thrilled to finally be away from everyone and their constant gossip about the quads. I've overheard way too many girls uttering their wishes to get the brothers alone today that I may end up screaming if I have to hear it anymore. And where has Cole been? I see the other three on a daily basis, but it's like he only shows up to be marked in his first class then magically disappears for the rest of the day. He's not even in the parking lot when it's time to leave.

My best friend smirks, tucking her arm through mine. "The football practices may be closed to students, but I'm on the newspaper."

"But I'm not."

"You're my friend; by default, that means you are too."

I snort and say, "Sooo?" I draw the word out.

Sam hauls me along as she shoves through the door leading us outside. The temperature's comfortable as we exit and I welcome the fresh air. Fall's right around the corner and it's one of my favorite times of the year. Winter here is disgustingly bitter, and spring always feels as if it will never arrive. Fall, however, is full of colored leaves, chilled breezes, pumpkin spiced lattes, cashmere sweaters, and cute leather jackets. I love it.

The football field's closest, the turf and surrounding grounds a lush, deep green. It looks so full and fluffy, it makes me want to sit on it in the sunshine. Sam leans in, sharing her devious plan. "Technically, I can be out here since it has to do with Academy sports. Everyone will be dying to read the sports column since it will no doubt feature information about HH's newest star players." Her eyes sparkle, entirely too excited for our own good.

With a groan, my hand hits my forehead. "How do you know they don't suck? Then this would be all for nothing. Plus Brandon's out here and you know how many times he's asked me to watch him practice. I don't want to give him the wrong idea."

She snorts. "That he has a chance, when we all know he doesn't? And also, for your information, I do my research when it comes to reporting accurate news. You, above all, know this."

"Annnd?" I whine.

She laughs at my dramatics and shares. "Those boys weren't

lying about winning trophies for their last school. They're talent is like NFL level and I'm going to be the first to report on it in our school paper."

"Of course it is," I mutter, tired of hearing how great they are. I wouldn't expect them to be anything less than perfect.

"According to previous articles, they're not considering sports in college at all. Athletic departments are in outrage over their brass balls to not even discuss options with various colleges," she shares as we watch them warming up on the flawless field. It's a benefit of being enrolled in a top-notch private school; our academy has the best equipment for everything, it seems. The schools weight room has won awards when compared to other schools. It's a bit obnoxious, but what can you expect from a top-tier school.

Tristan and Brent's frames are so enormous, they make a few of the other players look as small as freshman. "They probably won't even go. They strike me as a bunch of spoiled rich brats. Maybe they'll enroll to party and get laid, but I doubt they have med school or law school in their futures."

She jerks me, shaking me a little. "Hey, why are you being so negative? You're never like this. Did something happen with one of them? Every time we pass one of them they smile and say hi to you and don't think I'm the only one who's noticed that impressive fact either. The chicks around here are pissed that the quads give you so much more attention than any of them."

It's my turn to be stunned. "What? What are you talking about?"

She rolls her pretty eyes and flicks her dark hair over her shoulder. "Surely you've noticed..." She trails off, and I shake my head as my name's shouted. In fact, I've been doing my best to not notice things about them.

We both turn to look at the stands to see who could possibly be yelling at me, and I sputter. It's Axel waving at us. Or, I should say, he's waving at me since he's called my name. With a kind smile, I wave back and get elbowed in my side by my best friend.

"Bullshit! See what I mean? He hasn't even acknowledged me. I'm telling you, the girls around here are noticing it, too, and they're jealous." I turn to argue with her, and she bumps me again, nodding to the field. "He's not the only one showing you special attention either."

I follow her chin-lift, gazing out on the field where two beefy guys are waving our way as well. With an embarrassed sigh, I wave at them in return, knowing exactly who's big enough to fill out those uniforms. I don't need to see their name on the backs of their jerseys to realize it's Tristan and Brent. Not only that, but they're drawing the attention of all the other football players as well.

"This is a nightmare," I whisper, thinking of my plan I have set in stone. I'm supposed to be keeping my head down, studying hard and getting a scholarship, not drawing attention from the four most popular guys in school.

Sam yanks on my arm, carting me alongside the field toward the stands. When we get to the bleachers, Axel stands and greets, "Hey, Kresley." It's not lost on me that he doesn't say anything to Sam, and I'd already introduced her a few times previously. The guys always see my best friend buzzing around me, so this is feeling a bit awkward at the moment—like she's intruding.

"Hey, Axel," I raise my hand in a wave, though it's completely unnecessary. "You're not playing?" I already know he's not on the team, but it seems like the only thing I can come up with to say while his full attention is directed at me. Sam's the talker, not me unless it's with Brandon, then I'm a chatterbox.

"Nah, just out here watching my brothers and doing some homework. They're my ride home," he admits and shrugs.

I nod, mute. Apparently, I lose the ability to talk or else go directly in the opposite direction and ask personal questions.

Sam speaks up. "Oh, perfect! Kres was literally just telling me that she was planning to do the same thing. Great minds and all that." She then directs to me, "See? Now you finally have that study partner you were just wishing for!"

I could kill her right now. I never said that and being my best friend, she knows I prefer to do my work alone unless I'm tutoring someone.

She takes it a step further, earning a sharp look from me. "This works out perfect. I had something come up. Axel, you'll walk Kres to her car when you finish up, right? Gotta keep my bestie safe."

His forefinger nudges the thin ebony frame of his glasses up his nose a bit as he nods. "Of course. I won't let her walk alone. I promise to keep her safe."

"Thanks, Axel. You're a good guy, and we like good guys, don't we, Kresley?" She throws a wink my way as I secretly scowl back at her. She knows me well enough to notice my nostrils flaring at her antics. "I'll call you later." She grins wickedly, and I have no doubt she'll be blowing my phone up. She'll want every detail from the moment she walked off until I make it home.

Axel leans over, holding his hand out to help me up the few stairs between us. He's on the third row up, nothing I should be worried about falling down, but it's sweet all in the same. I place my palm in his, not wanting to be rude and turn the kindness away. Rather than letting go right away, he holds firm, pulling my messenger bag from my shoulder. He allows me to get seated before handing it over, and I'm so flustered I can't speak. He's not only good-looking and smart, but obviously, he's kind and has manners. This guy has me turning to goo in his palm, and I've barely sat down.

He's still holding my hand. I don't know if he's realized the simple fact, but it's the only thing I can think about. That small, intimate touch of his palm on mine has my head spinning. No matter how much I want to deny it, there's a spark—a big one. At least for me, there is, and by the way he stares at me like he's just as lost in me as I am in him, it makes me think he may feel it as well.

"Thank you," I eventually manage to choke out in a whisper.

His mouth kicks up, and he nods. His gaze lowers to our hands, and his smile grows. "Sorry, it appears that I've held your hand hostage."

I grin back like a giant idiot and shrug. He can keep it if he wants; I really wouldn't mind.

The spell's broken as Tristan shouts, "Hey, sugar plum! Watch me run this one, darling."

With a blink to clear the haze, I peer outward to the field, watching as Brent throws a perfect spiral that Tristan easily catches and runs down for a fake touchdown. The team cheers as what appears to be a play they'll soon be running falls in place.

"They're good," Axel murmurs, his thumb lightly rubbing over my knuckles.

I swallow before turning back to him. "They are. So, I heard you draw?" I change the subject to him, and his eyes light up. I'm guessing he's used to hanging back a bit in his brother's shadow, being they're jocks, and he's the smarter one. Little does he know, but I think smart is sexy.

"You were talking about me?" Axel questions and my cheeks heat with him calling me out.

I nod, and his expression turns from surprise to genuine interest. I've managed to catch all of their attention, and I don't know if this is a blessing or a curse. Whatever it is, I just hope they aren't my downfall. I have a feeling once you let them into your life, there's no turning back, and I just opened that door wide open.

Chapter Five

"Kresley!" My mother calls through the intercom system we have wired throughout the house. "You have a visitor."

I'd texted Sam, but apparently, she wanted to do this face-to-face. She knows better than to just show up though. My father's mood swings hit him out of nowhere, and God forbid something happen at work that angers him. We always feel the brunt of it, or I should say *I* feel the impact. I've tried to make it as clear as possible in the past to my best friend that she should always call me first unless it's important—like an emergency.

Placing a bookmark in my book to mark my spot, I close it and hop off my bed. No one comes over here besides Sam or my brother's friends, so I don't bother checking my hair or anything before jogging through the hallway and down the stairs. My mother comes into view first, looking the epitome of picture perfection and I'm expecting her to shoot me a look of disapproval. She wants to be informed at all times whenever I'm expecting company. Being wealthy means keeping up appearances and she may have had a hair out of place or something else just as scandalous. Rather than scorn, however, I'm met with a pleased smile—the type that definitely looks calculating. I'm thinking maybe it's Brandon now, instead of Sam.

"Mom?" I say and finally see who's waiting around the last curve of the grand staircase. It's definitely not anyone I'd expect to ever be stopping by. It's also not someone I want to see outside of school hours. I think about him enough without having him cloud up more of my mind.

"Tristan?" My brow creases, wondering what on earth he's doing here. This isn't your typical neighborhood; we don't ask to borrow sugar from the neighbor. If someone stops by unannounced, it's considered extremely rude, but you'd never guess that by the smile my mother wears. You'd think that this was Georgia and she'd just invited the neighborhood over for a barbecue and a slice of pie.

He flashes a devious grin. "We have a project to discuss, remember? You're the biology expert. I'm just you're ever grateful subject."

I could strangle him even if he is two or three heads taller than me and the size of a professional linebacker. I distinctly remember telling him that I wouldn't go over to his house after school, so I guess he decided to just show up here. How wonderful, said not me—ever.

"Right," I manage to grit free and turn to apologize to my mother. "Mom, I apologize for not informing you sooner we'd be having company. Everything seems to have not so conveniently slipped my mind." I flash Tristan and quick glare that promises he'll be hearing some choice words from me later when we're out of my mother's earshot.

"No worries, darling; I know how important studying after school is to you." She articulates smoothly.

I nearly choke as she takes Tristan's hand and then gives it an affectionate pat. She never speaks to me like this; she has to be up to something. In fact, I'd have to believe they both are. "The young Mr. de Lacharriere was just inviting us to have brunch with his family this Sunday. His father will be in town and wishes to meet the girl who's caught his son's eye."

Gag me, this is not happening.

I'm flat-out shocked. I was surprised to see him here and then to discover my mom so chummy with him, but now this too? They have to be joking, Tristan has girls draped over him nearly all day since arriving and they're never the same girls either. The asshole must've been buttering up my mother to get inside the house. She's not going to let me live this down either. This is undoubtedly his method of payback for me turning him down, and my mother will be more than eager to go along with whatever he's cooked up.

"We'd be obliged to host you at the club." His sparkling, stormy orbs meet mine, almost mockingly as if this is merely a game to him and he's made the next move. I wouldn't be surprised if it was…but if we show up at the club on Sunday and his family really isn't there, that embarrassment would make life more hellish around my father for the foreseeable future. He'll already be offended somewhat to be sitting with someone so wealthy; it'll makes our family look like peons in comparison if Sam's information is accurate. Why has Tristan decided to play cat-and-mouse games with me and make my life more miserable? Believe it or not, but his attention is not flattering.

"Thank you, Tristan." I offer a fake smile. I'm boiling inside, but it does the trick where my mother's concerned.

"We're honored," my mother repeats, preening at the invite. She loves that stuffy club full of pretentious, uptight assholes. "I'll make my exit and let you two visit." She flashes me another pleased smile, and I can read it perfectly without her uttering a word. She's commanding me to play nice whether I want to or not. So much for decking the good-looking boy in front of me, though 'boy' is not a term I'm sure is appropriate in his case. Tristan is massive, tall, and wide, muscles stacked with more muscles. He's nearly the same size as Brent, though he strikes me a bit more carefree and charismatic than his serious brother.

"Seriously?" I hiss, and he steps close enough that my chest nearly brushes against him with each breath I take. I feel like I just stepped into a showdown and was handed my ass on a platter.

"Cole warned you the first day of school that we run things. You should've listened," he retorts, cocky smirk fully in place. The bastard is serious about having his way and why I've struck his attention is completely lost on me. There's a full team of beautiful cheerleaders or a dance team at school who'd be dying to have his attention right now. Why can't he scurry off and go bother one of them?

"What does that have to do with anything to do with me?"

"I wanted you at my house tonight." He leans in a touch, staring at my chest and the rest of my curvy body unashamed.

An unladylike snort escapes me. "How's it feel to want, pretty boy?"

His mouth turns up into a grin; it's predatory and has me swallowing some of my courage down. "You're mine, Kresley, make no mistake. I'll forgive you this time, but the next time I tell you to be somewhere, you listen." I want to retort something snarky, but every thought besides Tristan de Lacharriere has seemed to have left my mind at the moment. His straightforward gaze pinned on me morphs into something resembling a jealous glower and my body shivers at his intensity, my stomach flip-flopping.

Bending closer, his lips lightly graze the lobe of my ear as he gravely rasps, "Keep your legs closed, Kres. I want my future wife untouched."

Drawing in a quick breath, my mind spins at his words. He can't be serious. With the parting look he flashes, I can't help but believe that he's dead serious. It can't be right; he's barely met me…I'm nobody in his world. What could he possibly want with me?

The rest of the week passes quickly without much happening thankfully, and it's enough to make me think Tristan has forgotten about me after all. We still sit next to each other in our shared biology class, but he's seemed to have backed off. One thing I have noticed, though, is that he hasn't had many girls hanging off of him like the first week of school. Don't get me wrong, there have been girls swarming him, but the only time I've caught any of them touching him is when he didn't notice me watching him. Could he have a change of heart toward the female population already and be serious about being interested in me?

Axel, on the other hand, is quickly becoming my new study partner. He's basically a genius, I've discovered. I seriously doubt he needs my help at all. If anything, I hold him back. He seems to enjoy helping me, though, and I've found that cramming with him has made the work seem less challenging and overwhelming. I want the best grades as possible for that scholarship and being around someone so smart is a bit inspiring. Not only that, but Axel is genuinely kind. He's sincere, sweet, and not self-centered. I find myself looking for him whenever I'm in the halls to wave a quick hello and see how his day's going. Now, he's one brother whose attention I could get used to having, not that I need to complicate things when I have a plan to stick to.

Another bonus when it comes to him is that girls aren't so forward all the time, acting desperate for his attention. Sure he's just as gorgeous as his brothers, but he's not the "in your face" gorgeous like the others so easily seem to be. Axel hides his calm, ashen irises behind his square-ish raven-framed Clark Kent glasses and his quiet, shy demeanor doesn't easily draw girls in. If anything, I'm sure most of the school thinks he's stuck up, but if you get to know him, you'll discover that isn't the case at all. He's muscular in his own sense, but more on the long and lean side versus his bulky brothers. He's lifted my messenger bag full of books before and I've seen his biceps flex with the motion, so I know he's hiding so much more under his bland navy and black academy uniform. I try not to go around thinking of my classmate's body, yet I find myself gazing at him and wondering if he has a six pack under his finely-pressed, dark blue button-up shirt.

Sunday rolls around, and I find myself on the way to the infamous club. I'm off to have brunch with Tristan and whoever else decides to join from his family. Part of me is terrified they won't show up. I'd put the brunch to the back of my mind, distracted with the day-to-day routine, but then yesterday my mother insisted we go shopping and get mani's and pedi's. She's still lecturing me as we pull up to the gates leading into the prestigious club my father often enjoys visiting. I'd taken golf lessons here when I was younger but found it to be incredibly boring. I never understood how my father found so much enjoyment out of something as mundane as golfing.

"This is how futures are decided, Kresley," my mother chides accordingly, and I turn off to the side, rolling my eyes.

"There's nothing going on like that between Tristan and me. I've told you that already; this meeting doesn't make any sense," I argue even though I don't want to irritate my father. I need her to understand that this brunch isn't going anywhere now nor in the future.

"Nonsense," she huffs and bulldozes on. "His father wouldn't have requested brunch if there wasn't an impending engagement to be discussed."

Her disclosure has my hand flying to my chest, my mouth dropping open as I gasp in outrage. My heart suddenly feels as if there's a wild horse stomping through my chest. This isn't a part of my plan; it was never even a consideration. Sure, we're wealthy, but I never once believed we were on the level of discussing premature marriage options. I'm supposed to get a scholarship and move far away from here, all on my own. I'm so close to being out of my parents' house and away from their unhealthy lifestyle. This can't be happening to me right now.

My father speaks for the first time since we've left, his voice commanding, leaving no room for argument. "Axel de Lacharriere is Tristan's grandfather. He's the second wealthiest man in France, the thirteenth richest man in America and you want to rebuff any potential future that's linked with their family? Are you completely stupid, Kresley? You'll be a good girl, and if anyone in that family so much as whispers their interest in your direction, you'll roll over and oblige immediately. You will not embarrass me or else I'll make sure you never have a happy moment for the rest of your life, little girl. If that boy has a ring, you slide that rock on your finger immediately and smile like it's the best fucking thing in the entire world, because it is."

Tears attempt to fight their way to my eyes, but I choke the sob back. Meeting my father's hateful stare in the rearview mirror, I nod and whisper, "Yes, sir." I know I have nothing to worry about; Tristan wouldn't be serious about dating me, let alone marrying me. The tears are because when my father discovers that my mother has put this false hope into his head, it'll be hell to pay at home. My mother may catch some of his anger, but I'll be the one shouldering the load because he'll blame me for screwing up somehow. He's precisely the reason why I don't have foolish wishes clouding my head in the first place. My life is a cold dose of reality when it concerns him, and regardless of what he may believe, I'm not stupid. I'm working my tail off on my grades, so I never have to rely on him again. I want as far from Harvard Academy and this town as possible.

We unload right in front of the main entryway doors, and the valet takes the keys from my father to park the Range Rover. My dad typically drives a sporty car, but he likes to drive my mom's family vehicle when we go out like this. He has this ridiculous belief that it makes him appear more like a doting father and husband. There's not an ounce of blood in him that screams family man; I know that for a fact. I find myself often wondering why he doesn't just shove us all into his tiny McLaren since being rich seems to be more important than any of us. I'm sure I come off as bitter to some, but I promise that's not the case. I'm grateful for his money taking up most of his time. I'm just not happy with how it's made him into such a rotten human being.

The thick, oversized glass doors to the luxurious club are opened for us, and my father's greeted by name from the host. It's their job to memorize every card holder, but my father spends enough time here I'm sure they're actually familiar with him.

"The de Lacharrieres are waiting for you, sir." The host gestures toward the posh dining area, and my muscles tighten. Tristan wasn't lying after all; someone with their last name is indeed waiting for us. My gut churns that this is a disaster waiting to happen, but it's like a train wreck, and I'm tied to the tracks. I can't escape no matter how I may attempt to struggle out of my bonds.

We approach the back corner that's considered to be a coveted private seating placement, and five tall males stand to greet us. A petite, young blonde woman who looks close to my age scrambles to her feet at the last moment, standing next to Mr. de Lacharriere. There's no mistaken who he is. The boys look like perfect younger replicas of him. Their father clearly has dominant genes to not only have one son but four of them. Then to add in the fact that the resemblance is uncanny, there's four spitting images of the powerful man himself.

The host introduces our fathers before scurrying away to be seen and not heard. The older men shake hands, then acknowledge their significant others before the attention is turned in my direction.

Tristan's father has me blushing as he peppers a fake kiss on each of my cheeks and clasps my hand between his large, warm palms. He's handsome, smells nice and reminds me of all four boys wrapped into one—he's a dangerous combination. "You must be the young lady my son won't stop talking about. I can see why now... You are absolutely stunning, my dear." He doesn't look at me like a father should; his gaze takes me in more like a potential conquest.

I swallow and offer up a too wide smile that I'm sure comes off more as a toothy grimace. I'm flattered, really. He seems quite charming. I'm just worried that if I screw this up or there isn't a ring involved that the rest of my life will completely suck. I didn't begin this week wanting or even considering marriage, but suddenly it seems like the only thing I can think of, the only thing to save me from my family. I don't want to be married, but my father does, and in this life, that's all that really matters. I'm a pawn to be traded as needed in grown men's games.

"Thank you, sir." I manage to stick to my ingrained manners and mumble.

Tristan rounds the table, the bold move seemingly like a premeditated production of sorts. He shake's my father's hand first, and then presses a light kiss to my mother's knuckles. Lastly, he stops in front of me. "My love," he proclaims, and I grit my teeth. This whole charade is lies, and I can't stand it. I keep my mouth shut, offering him a fake, closed-mouth smile. "You look as beautiful as always."

There's a flash from the side window, and I instantly recognize that this is a publicity setup. These people have so much nerve and glancing in my father's direction, I catch the wide smile on his lips. He loves this so far. In fact, he'd probably parade me outdoors so they could get a better angle on this entire ridiculous situation.

"Thank you, Tristan." I choke out the tight, robotic reply. At this point, I'm going on etiquette alone and repeating thank you for practically everything.

He holds both of my hands in his palms, his gaze twinkling with some sort of plot I'm sure I won't want to take part in.

Tristan's father interrupts us further. "Shall we toast?" Everyone's still standing up around the table, and it feels so awkward and completely staged to me. "We have much to be excited for," the older man boasts, and I try to tug my hands away. Tristan won't allow it though, clamping his hold tighter.

He speaks up, almost as if this entire morning has been rehearsed already. It has me on edge. I don't like this; it all feels so planned and fake. "Father, excuse me, but with your blessing, I'd like to make an announcement...or shall I say, ask a question."

Mr. de Lacharriere beams at his son, the devious asshole standing before me. "Of course, Tristan. Let's turn this into a celebration."

It's the only encouragement he needs, and Tristan drops to one knee beside the table. The dining room's silent as all of the surrounding guests have quieted, their nosiness getting the best of them. Usually, you at least pretend to talk while you eavesdrop, but not for this apparently.

I think I'm going to puke. Like literally upchuck all over this gorgeous boy's clothes and shoes. That'd be my luck.

Tristan releases one hand, keeping a tight grip on the other as he fishes out a small ivory box from the inside pocket of his suit jacket. Using his thumb, he pops the top open, a massive diamond glinting at me in the process. He flashes his perfectly straight, bright white teeth in what some would say is a nervous smile. It's not. I can read him like an open book. This is one big script for him. The worst part of all is that I can do absolutely nothing about any of it but simply accept and agree. "Forgive me for not planning something more special, I just can't wait a moment longer," he continues, and I have to stop myself from rolling my eyes. "You've caught me completely off guard, a whirlwind of love enveloping me when I wasn't expecting it. No one could shy from your beauty or that brilliant mind, and you've fully ensnared me from all others. Kresley, my love, please do me the honor and allow me to take care of you. Your future will have no limits by my side; you'll make me the happiest man alive. Please, please do me the honor of becoming my wife."

I still feel like I want to vomit. My stomach rolls with what he's just done. I've known him two weeks, and that's pushing it. Sharing one biology class with someone is hardly considered as knowing them. I suppose I should be thankful; in this rich world, many never meet each other until these things have already been decided. If I'm honest with myself, I'm feeling a bit betrayed that Axel hasn't said anything about this. We've seen each other every day this past week, and he never mentioned or even hinted that Tristan was serious about meeting up this weekend and what I should be expecting.

I swallow down the bile threatening to spew everywhere and jerk a disappointed nod in response. A tear falls, but Tristan holds me tightly, not allowing me to wipe it away. I'm sure it fits perfectly, him on his knees with some ridiculous speech while I stand here tearing up. They aren't happy tears, more like the final seal on my coffin. My life is no longer mine, but then I guess it never was, to begin with. I was the fool to have believed differently.

He slips on the massive diamond before getting to his feet. Leaning in, he whispers mockingly, "You belong to the de Lacharrieres now. Told you that you'd be mine."

My head feels fuzzy as his fingers grab my chin roughly and his lips press to mine, then everything goes completely black.

Chapter Six

My mother was more than happy to proclaim that my passing out was due to an overabundance of excitement. There wasn't an ounce of truth to it, though I never once attempted to correct her. I wouldn't dare to ever bring it up. My father had commanded me to be the impeccable, willing victim, after all, and I wasn't about to give him any reason to extend his fury on our family further. The less ammunition he has against us, the better.

The entire situation felt like one colossal sham of a production. I wanted no involvement whatsoever of the engagement or that flashy family full of testosterone-filled good-looking men. I tried like hell to hide the ostentatious ring upstairs, but my mother wasn't having it. There's no way I wanted to wear it to school and allow everyone to see what'd happened over the weekend. It's bad enough that it'll probably show up in a paper somewhere.

Now, here I am, headed to lunch wearing an enormous diamond ring on my finger that's so big I may as well have gotten my forehead tattooed. The quads have left me on my own so far today, and every time I've made eye contact with Brandon, my heart aches. My best guy friend stares at me with a resounding sadness as if I just slit my throat and told him he'll never be able to love another. I'm not in love with him in the slightest, but I do care for him. He's been a good friend to me nearly my entire life. I know he loves me more than I deserve, and his pain from my unofficial engagement is unfair. I don't want him to hurt or be sad on account of me or anyone else.

I don't want to marry Tristan, but I'd never admit that, even to Brandon. I couldn't handle giving him any false hope only to snatch it away the day my last name becomes de Lacharriere. I'm not stupid; I know it'll happen eventually. The diamond glinting on my finger cements it in stone.

Entering the lunchroom, I casually stride toward my usual table to sit and place my order when my wrist is snatched. It catches me off guard, and I nearly stumble. The secure grip holds firm, and I follow the offending limb to none other than my betrothed. Taking a breath, I silently pray for patience, so I don't mess this up and attract Father's anger.

"This is your new seat," Tristan proclaims, nodding to the chair next to his. He's in his neatly pressed academy shirt sans blazer. The Harvard Academy signature coat is folded neatly over the chair across from him. Of course, he'd take up extra seats for his personal items; he seems to have no awareness for others around him other than his three brothers. If this is any indication to how our future will be, I know I'll be miserable—maybe not as much as living at home, but miserable all the same.

Jerking my wrist free, I flash a sarcastic smile. "I have a seat already, right over there with my friends." I point to the table where Sam and Brandon sit with their heads together in a hushed, in-depth conversation that I'd bet money on is about me and my newly-acquired accessory. "That's been my place for the past few years and will be for the remainder of this one."

His handsome face twists with a scoff. "This is the de Lacharriere table," he states. "You'll sit next to your future husband or else I'll make sure your friend is kicked off the team," he threatens and a war wages inside my chest.

Both of my best friends will be miffed that I'm not sitting with them. It'll be me making a silent statement to the room that I'm not comfortable with making. On the flip side, I know how much Brandon absolutely loves playing football and needs it in his life. Anyone can see how talented he truly is when he's on the field, and it would be devastating to him if he were kicked off. I couldn't live with myself if he loses his first love on account of me.

My conflicted stare meets Tristan's victorious gleam as he stands. Snatching my hand back into his much bigger grip, he brings my hand to his mouth. He presses a kiss to the knuckle above my shiny new engagement ring. Every single person is paying attention to us—their eyes glued to the scene before them. It doesn't take a genius to know exactly what he's doing. Tristan just announced our status to the entire academy without saying a word aloud.

After a beat, Tristan uses his free hand to pull the seat he'd indicated outward. He directs my hand downward, making me follow suit and sit where he wants me to. It's been one day, yet he's already moving me around like his personal puppet. I don't know whether to be frightened or not. While my father is physically abusive, Tristan is manipulative in his own sense.

I'm positively steaming inside, anger rolling through me. It's times like this that the pavement calls to me. I need to run these emotions out before I do something rash. I'd gotten up early today and ran a few miles, but I need it again and right now. Swallowing, I straighten myself in my seat, the server coming to my side immediately. They've always been good, but never quite this quick. Another perk of being filthy rich, I suppose—you get waited on hand and foot, or else people lose their jobs with a snap of your fingers.

Assholes, I think to myself but thankfully manage to keep the comment silent.

Ordering my usual, the baked chicken and rice pilaf, I wait for someone to interrupt and tell me what I'm now allowed to eat as well. Surprisingly, that didn't happen, and I'm able to have what I want.

A glower shutters over my face as I scan each boy sitting around the table. They're comfortable, looking like they own the place. Even Axel feels the depth of my fury as I stare him down. I was foolish enough to previously believe he was a potential friend and ally.

Cole smirks, mouthing "beba" when my glare lands on him. I can't believe I thought that Cajun boy accent was hot when I first stumbled upon him standing under the tree watching me stretch. He may be gone all the time, but he's clearly in on this with his brothers. I highly doubt any of them do anything without each of them being fully aware of what's going down. They're far too devious for my liking, and I'm not entirely sure what to do with the lot of them.

Brent ignores me, though I've grown used to it. He always acts like I don't exist, so I try to return the favor. I still don't understand why we have to sit here like one big fake happy family when last week they didn't seem to have a problem sitting with me at my usual table. It's like they met me and then decided one day that they'd make my life hell from now on.

Not being able to hold myself back any longer from remarking, I hiss, "Holding court, are we? A little pompous, don't you think?" I'm rich too, but the way they sit with their noses in the air, you can feel the wealth pouring from them. It's not classy in the slightest.

Cole chuckles, flashing an amused glance at Tristan, "Mm-mm, mon beba has claws, no?"

Axel mutters, "She'll need them to be one of us."

My drink is set in front of me, and I quickly thank the server before gulping some of the water down. Tristan smiles, but I see right through the insincerity of it. "Maybe we are holding court. So what, we're at the top of the food chain. Look around sugar plum, everyone knows their place."

My angry stare scans across the room, and everyone randomly peeks over at our table, longing in their gaze. "My family has less money than half of these people," I point out. "I'm in the middle, so clearly I don't belong here either. I could leave if you'd be more comfortable around your own kind."

Tristan leans in close, his warm breath hitting my lobe, making me flush with goosebumps. The damn things easily tattle on my reaction to him when that's the last thing I want him or anyone else to be aware of. "As long as that expensive rock is weighing down your finger, you'll be better than all of them. In fact, your future last name alone makes you better than them all combined, fiancée."

Drawing in a stunned breath, I sip another cold drink of my water. Father wasn't lying when he sprouted off about their net worth. That was their grandfather's though, so I didn't think their father, and by default, the boys were that wealthy as well. I don't bring anything to their table, there's no reason they should be demanding I marry one of them. Dad is thrilled, of course, and Tristan's father was already boasting about how I'm his new daughter by the time we ended our brunch yesterday. It's incredibly unsettling, and there's not a damn thing I can do about any of it. I'm just a pawn in some rich men's games. Even with Tristan, I'm another move to make.

By Thursday my week has only gotten tougher. Everyone—and I mean every single person, including the faculty—knows about Tristan and me. The guys who never seemed to notice me much before suddenly avoid me like I have the plague. In the moments I do accidently catch one of them staring, they're looking at me like I'm a damn unicorn or something. You'd swear I'd shown up to school in lingerie and it's the first time they've ever been acquainted with Victoria's Secret. Though I suppose that brand isn't even good enough anymore being linked to this prestigious family. Tristan had several boxes hand delivered to my house yesterday, one of them being from an exclusive, outrageously expensive French boutique. I fought with my mom over it all, but she demanded I wear one of the silky bras today and let Tristan know how thoughtful it was of him to send me gifts.

Puke.

I'll admit, I've never felt something so soft on my boobs before, but I absolutely refuse to even hint to Tristan that I'm wearing any of it. In fact, the next time I see him, I'm telling him it didn't fit, so I donated it to the homeless. I don't care how good-looking or how much his smile makes my stomach twist in knots, I'm not going to make this engagement easy on him. They should've chosen someone else to be their newest pet.

I've always been someone who gets along with pretty much everyone. At least, I thought so. I give that credit to attending camp each summer and being around people who have a shared love for the outdoors. This week, however, you'd think I was the biggest asshole around. The girls have started making comments when I walk by. It began low-keyed from a few of the wealthiest females. Since then, it's warped to basically every girl I come in contact with.

I'm beginning to feel like I'm losing my mind or something, as the name calling, ugly looks, and rude remarks never happen when Tristan's by my side. The last thing I want is to need his presence for anything, but walking through the halls is much more pleasant when he's pretending to be the committed fiancé. Cole wasn't joking when he said they'd run the school. They came in, and within a few days were crowned academy royalty by my peers. I guess by default that makes me "royalty" as well, though I don't want it. I'm not better than anyone, and I never will be.

I'm finishing up our athletics class, and I can't get out soon enough. You'd think I was a terrible person with the many glares and snooty remarks I keep trying to brush off. At what point will all of this stop? I've never been a subject of bullying and hate before. Why on earth would people be so cruel? Sad to say, but if Sam were here, she'd be the first one to stand up and tell them all to fuck right off. I wish I had Sam's woman balls, and in a sense

I do, but I'm trying to just ignore these mean girls to see if they'll get bored. I'm trying to be patient and not reinforce their nastiness with my own.

My back crashes into the wall of the girl's locker room. I'm right inside the door, trapped in the enclosed walkway before all of the lockers, changing area, and showers. There was some whispered name calling during athletics, but I let it roll off me as I have all day. I don't tend to be a very confrontational person, though I haven't needed to be in the past. I got through my shower like usual, and then there were more hurtful things thrown my way. Bitch, whore, slut, trash, et cetera—the usual name-calling, but I couldn't for the life of me figure out why I suddenly deserve them. Tears trailed over my face while under the hot spray of my shower, contemplating the treatment I'd received lately. I try to be strong, but sometimes I have to let it all out, especially if I can't pound it out on the pavement in a long run.

It's not like I'm sleeping around; technically, I'm still a virgin compared to all of them. One time at camp last year and then nothing else isn't my idea of being an academy whore amongst them. No one knows that business, as it's none of their concern what I do and don't do. Now, I'm engaged to one boy who I haven't even had sex with, and yet I'm the whore? How does that make any sense? People's logic is mind-boggling to me sometimes.

Devon Monteith slams me against the wall again—my head bouncing off the hard surface and making me cry out. Pain explodes behind my eyes. I grit my teeth to stop the tears from falling as her fist flies into my stomach. I've done nothing to deserve this treatment, especially from girls I've known for years and have never had a touch of bad blood with. Apparently, that's changed now, and I really wish someone would clue me in. Is it jealousy? They can have Tristan; I don't want him. I'm just doing what's expected of me by my family.

Devon's a head taller than me, and that's saying something as I'm considered relatively tall for a girl. She's never been so hateful toward me in the past either. In fact, we've always been friendly toward one another. Now it's like she's been possessed and I can't seem to escape her in gym class or the hallway. It's ironic because if Tristan or one of the other guys is with me when I see her, she acts like a damn angel. Apparently, there's nothing angelic about her whatsoever as her face twists in hate, spewing her unwarranted rage today.

"Give me that ring!" she screams manically, repeating her demand.

"Ugly Academy whore!" Her group of friends yells behind her.

The gym doors are thrown open, banging into the opposite wall from the force. The noise booms into the area, startling my heart even more than the crazy chicks trying to hurt me. My hand's wrapped around the massive diamond weighing my finger down, trying to stop her from jerking it free from my hand. It had to cost a fortune, and there's no way I'll let anyone take it willingly when I know the repercussions I'll face for it.

In the next blink, Brent's furious, hulking presence is behind Devon, towering over her. He grabs a fistful of her hair, ripping her head back until she falls to the ground yelling in protest. "Get out!" he thunders, and I shrink down, attempting to make myself smaller. It's unlike me, but I've been around Father in his fury. I know when to stay out of an irate man's way.

The group of girls who'd been taunting me behind Devon scurries out as if their asses are on fire. Brent's breathing heavily, each pant releasing a little bit of his anger as he attempts to reel in his control. His commanding sapphire irises flick over me from top to bottom assessing the potential damage. He's scary and beautiful like this. It makes me want to reach out and touch him. I won't though; it's not the time or my place to do so.

I'm an utter mess, even if I did just finish showering and putting on my Harvard Academy uniform. I can feel it. My cheeks are streaked with confused and annoyed tears, my body trembles with the pain rolling through my muscles from Devon's torment. My head pounds with an oncoming headache. I'll need some Tylenol soon, or else it'll stick around for the rest of the day.

Brent steps forward. His hand lifts to my uniform, straightening out my disheveled clothes and I flinch. I can't help it; I just witnessed him throwing a girl to the floor by her hair. Granted it was to help me, but it still has me shaken up inside. I've been hit by my father far too many times to take the brunt off my younger brother and mom, not to mention Dad directs it at me to begin with.

I don't know Brent well enough to distinguish if he shares in his need to hit people like Father does. I don't get that feeling from him, however. If anything, it's quite the opposite. He has this sense of calm and control that he makes me feel safe when he's around. I wasn't expecting him today, and the violence triggered my body's self-preservation.

Once my clothes are to his satisfaction, he meets my teary, confused gaze. His glower is so powerful it has me drawing in a quick breath, not out of newfound fear but because he's so beautifully dangerous in the moment that I can't help myself. He may appear to be the same as his brothers, but there are so many differences between them all that I could never get them mixed up. Brent is definitely the oldest; he's the powerhouse that takes care of his family when needed. He's broody and quiet, the buff quad that you don't see coming until he's ready for you to and it's far too late to do anything about it.

"You okay?" Brent murmurs and I jerk with a short nod. He huffs, "You can't let them hit you like that." He's giving me orders like I'm another person he has to take care of, like his brothers. My heart rate beats double time with his sole attention; it does that when I'm faced with any of them and we're alone. It's strange and confusing to feel this way with four boys, especially when they all resemble each other. It feels wrong in a sense, but I can't seem to stop.

"Th-they surprised me," I admit with a chastised croak.

I clear my throat, watching with rapt attention as Brent licks his lips. The move instantly has me thinking of his tempting mouth on mine. He has a full, pouty mouth, with a bit of a natural downward pull to his lips making him appear to be frowning. They'd be perfect to kiss. I know it. As if reading my thoughts, his hand lifts, his thumb lightly stroking over my wet, bottom lip I'd been biting on and not realized. He stares intently at the spot he grazes, lost in the moment. I want him to kiss me so badly I can't breathe. The air's stuck in my lungs as I wait for his next move.

With his next blink, Brent's walls fall back into place, and he takes a step away, putting some respectable distance between us. His massive paw engulfs my bicep, carting me along with him through the gym doors. It happens so quickly, my feet are moving before it registers he's taking me to my next class. I don't need to be manhandled, especially after being put through the ringer by Devon and her cronies.

"What are you doing?" I whisper as we head through the hall, students openly gaping at him carting me around like a bratty toddler. No one says anything about it, however, as his glare is threatening enough.

With a growl, he explains, "I'm taking you to your fucking class before you get into any more trouble. Try to stay out of the girl's way if you aren't going to stick up for yourself. I have other things to do besides saving your ass."

I'm about to retort that I've never asked for his help in the first place, not even once when Brent jerks me to a stop. We're at my next class. My mouth opens, and he barks, "Get inside." Then the moody asshole spins on his heel and heads in the opposite direction.

The instructor's brow rises as I meet her curious gaze. She takes in my disheveled appearance without commenting on it, probably thinking I'm giving it up to the four of the entitled bastards and I hastily slide into my seat. Thankfully, she goes into her lecture garnering the class's attention once more and saves me further from my embarrassing state. I can't believe he just did that in front of everyone without a care in mind. What would his father think if he caught wind of students witnessing us like that? Would he even care? I'm assuming that'd be a no or else Brent would keep a lid on his temper better. One thing's for sure, I have my hands full when it comes to Brent, Tristan, Cole, and Axel. I have a sinking suspicion that won't be the first time they embarrass me…or save me.

My day only gets worse as I'm bumped into in the hallway and called variations of slut or whore by numerous peers. Devon and the other girls from gym class quickly spread around details of the locker room altercation and how I'm going to get my ass kicked again if I don't give up my new status with the quad. Other students throw in their own variations of threats, making me feel sick about the entire situation. I've never experienced anything like it, even when I was younger and on the chunky side. I'd caught some rude looks and such back then, but not to this level of hatefulness. Sam's attempted several times to defend me as well, by throwing her elbow into anyone who's gotten too close, but it's not helping. If anything, it only makes me feel worse, my heart aching with guilt over the snide remarks thrown her way also for being my best friend.

"It's jealousy," she claims as the day finally finishes and we escape out the back door near the football field again. I don't want Tristan to think I'm coming out to watch him because I'm not. This route was the quickest way to get away from the students determined to harass me. I don't want Sam having to deal with any more of this nonsense today either.

"That's absurd, Sam; they have no reason to be jealous of me. Majority of the tormentors today are wealthier than my family! I have nothing they could want…think about it."

Her long, dark hair glints in the sunshine as she huffs, "You're so oblivious, Kres. God! This is exactly why you need me by your side, and I won't let you run off and hide alone like I know you want to. The girls around here have always been intimidated when it comes to you, and you've taken it up a bar with your new status.

You're the whole package babe—beauty *and* brains. Majority of the chicks attending Harvard Academy are on the short list for boob implants and nose jobs in hopes their dear ol' daddies will marry them off to some old rich guy. The only consolation they have is if the guy croaks early and they get compensated with wealth and a young, hot pool boy."

A scoff escapes as I roll my eyes. There's no way that can be true. "I'm practically invisible, or at least I was before now. Besides, Devon and her friends are hot; they can't be intimidated by me."

"Plastic bimbos," she grumbles and rolls her eyes. "Are you kidding me? Didn't you notice how last year half of the females at the academy showed up on day one with lavender-tinted hair? It wasn't because all the other colors at the salon were gone." She shoots me a look believing it's enough substantial evidence to prove her point.

"Well, I've never noticed it before, and I thought the hair was because of a trend. Besides, when they left me alone before, it was exactly what I wanted. I need to concentrate on classes and get that scholarship. It's my main priority."

"Your dad will pay for school, Kres. He already said he will, and you should take it. It's the least he can do."

I nod because she's completely right. "Yeah and he'll also be picking which college I attend if he does end up paying. I don't want him to have any more power over my life then he already does."

She shrugs, waving my worry off. "So he picks it... Would it really be that bad? I could enroll in the same college or one that's nearby. Maybe it wouldn't be as terrible as you think it would be."

Sam's wrong, but I don't have a chance to reply as Axel stands in my way along the path leading to the student parking lot.

"Can I talk to you?" Axel interrupts, appearing a bit nervous.

My gaze snaps to his as Sam shoots me a teasing wink and

waves at the throng of practicing football players. "I'll call you later," she calls not breaking stride and leaves me behind.

I move to sidestep the intelligent quad in my way, but he quickly follows, holding his hands out. "Please, Kresley. Give me a moment…just one…to explain. I tried to speak to you in class earlier, but you left before I had a chance to pack my stuff up. This can't wait any longer."

"I don't have anything to say to you right now, Axel." It pains me to cut off our friendship so early on, but I'm upset he didn't at least think to warn me about his brother's intentions and underhanded actions.

"I do, please. I can make it quick, just hear me out." His palms lightly reach out and cup my elbows. His movement brings us closer together, encompassing us into our own little bubble. There may be people all around on the practice fields, but it's like Axel has expertly cut them all off from the two of us. "I want to apologize."

A disbelieving snort escapes me as my gaze drops his to stare off toward the empty bleachers. We don't have regular football stands that you find in other high schools. Our field is state of the art with individual seating in rows. Each placement provides plenty of leg room and comfortable padding wrapped in outdoor material. It dries quickly if it rains, is easy to clean and doesn't mold, because clearly wealthy people can't stand to be out of their comfort zone even when it comes to football. Not that I can complain. I've sat in these stands my fair share of times, and I've enjoyed the posh comforts over visiting other high school stadiums.

Axel leans in and confesses softly, "I'm being serious, Kresley. I don't want this tension between us. I don't like having you upset with me."

Briefly closing my eyes tightly, I exhale and meet his pewter irises. "I figured out of the four of you, you'd be the one I could actually trust. It's stupid. I've barely met you, and I should've known better. I have myself to blame for being blind and so easily trusting, not you."

Axel's perfect white teeth bite down on his plump bottom lip. He's pensive as if he has so much to say but isn't sure if he should or how to breach it all with me. "It's not stupid, not in the least and you can trust me. I want you to; I want you to feel like you can come to me at any time with any subject. Even if it has only been two weeks, it feels longer to me. You're not the only one in this that feels like they've grown close. You're my friend, Kresley," he admits, and I agree. "I didn't know that was going to happen at brunch. I was caught off guard as well," Axel shares, his voice coming out in a near whisper.

Is he afraid that someone may overhear us having this conversation? I flick my gaze around, but no one seems to be paying us any attention. His brothers are MIA as well; Tristan and Brent are out running around on the field, busy with football practice. My friend Brandon left as well after seeing me at lunch again. He's not out here with the rest of them at practice, so there's really no reason for Axel to be so quiet.

Unless he's being sincere about his remorse and me being wounded really is weighing on him heavily. Maybe he's telling the truth about feeling the same way I did about our fast friendship? And now if this whole charade goes through with me marrying Tristan, I could use someone on my side in his family, an ally. His brothers are so moody they give me whiplash and overwhelm me. Having Axel as a friend and supporter could definitely help me get through the future if necessary. Plus, I like him; he's kind and doesn't seem to base talking to me only because he wants something from me. We probably have more in common than I do with any of the other quads.

"I felt ambushed on Saturday," I confess, deciding to give him a shot. "We showed up, and I thought Tristan had been joking when he extended the invitation to my mother. I didn't believe your family would be there, nonetheless that he'd be proposing to me. I was shocked, and to be honest, I was embarrassed and angry."

With a jerk of his head, he pulls me to his chest. My hands fall to his torso, feeling more strength there than I ever imagined. He may not play football or other organized school sports, but he must regularly work out with his brothers. Axel's solid, and his sturdy grip feels soothing and sincere while wrapped around me. His nose tucks into my hair at the top of my head as he comforts and reassures me, "I'm sorry, Kresley. I don't ever want you feeling that way. I do value you, and I want you to be confident that you can always count on me."

Tilting my head back, I take in his dilated, serious stare and his handsome features, offering up a genuine smile in return. He's a good guy and I' being too hard on him. It's not fair for me to take my anger and confusion out on him when he clearly doesn't deserve it. "Thank you."

He breaks out in a pleased grin, the sight causing my breath to catch. "Want to go to my house? We haven't studied together this week, and I've missed it," he offers, reminding me of an eager puppy—a big, gorgeous one, but still.

Taking a step back, he releases me as I gesture out toward the field chuck full of sweaty football players and various other athletes. "Don't you have to wait for Brent and Tristan to finish with their practice?"

"No." He shakes his head, flashing a smile. "I usually wait for them to give me a ride home, but if you don't mind, you could drive us?"

"Oh, definitely. I didn't realize, or I'd have offered sooner. Let's go...I mean, if you're ready?" I retract, not wanting to come off as bossy. That's Sam's personality, not mine, and besides, I'm sure he deals with that enough being around Brent, Tristan, and Cole.

He nudges his glasses up a bit on his nose and nods, turning to pack up his textbook and academy-issued tablet. "Lead the way, my dear Lois Lane." He places his messenger bag strap over his shoulder and then reaches for mine to do the same. He's a gentleman, unlike his pushy brothers.

The nickname still manages to give me butterflies in my abdomen. The flutters hit me even heavier inside when Axel's light touch comes to rest on the middle of my back as he follows me to my Jaguar. My feelings are already evolving with the guys, and I've only known them for two weeks. Throw in a touch here and there from them, and I'm quickly turning to putty in their hands.

Chapter Seven

I've known the boys for over a month before it starts to hit me that they've fully integrated themselves into my life. Tristan is a given, of course, since he's put an engagement ring on my finger for the entire world to see. Fiancé or not, I think he's a spoiled dick most the time. I'm still stuck with him, though. There's no way I can be rude or try to ditch him for fear of repercussions from Dad.

Brent has filled the makeshift role of my personal protector, but only when he finds it to be convenient for him. There are times when he just huffs with annoyance and passes by when someone is picking on me. He said I need to stick up for myself, but I've been trying to ignore everyone rather than have an altercation. Of course, I could speak up, but what if the locker room incident becomes a repeat occasion? I'd rather deal with the occasional mean girl or hateful remark versus physical abuse or groups ganging up on me at the same time.

Sam wants to help out, but I can't drag her into this too much. What kind of friend would I be if I expected her to be involved, and they all start to turn on her as well? That's not fair in the slightest, and I refuse to have her fight my battles. Brandon has barely spoken two words to me, so I don't know if he's truly aware of how bad things have gotten. He's another friend I would never expect to put himself at jeopardy for my well-being.

Cole doesn't speak to me often. When he does break the silent treatment, it's usually to remind me that his family now owns me. Another of his favorite things to say is how the quads run the school, and they'll eventually run the country if they should desire. I'm not going to attempt to argue with him over it, because it will get me nowhere. Besides, Cole's not lying, his family *does* possess me as far as Father is concerned. You'd think the four boys had hung the moon or something to that degree.

Axel, however, has become my daily study partner and friend. I can confide in him and be confident he won't throw me under the bus with his siblings. Nearly every day, we skip out on watching and waiting around for football practice to be over. Instead, we opt to hole up in his room or else take over the kitchen. Axel and I have made it into our own personal cooking class. I've never been around a boy I've felt so comfortable with, and that frightens me because I find myself wanting to get even closer to him. It's worse when he touches me. The light brushes here and there have me craving more, and that can't happen.

Take today, for example. Axel and I got into a useless argument over the average time people are able to hold their breath under water. To prove me wrong, he declared that we were going swimming to rule out any dispute. It was completely dumb, but we had so much fun just goofing off together. We don't have a normal friendship like we should; it's more than that.

Now, Axel lays spread out and relaxed on his bed, completely at ease with me in his space. His hair's wet and messy, making him appear disheveled and ridiculously sexy while I peruse his room. I've done it many times by now, but I can't help myself and decide to tease him some. We're finally at that level that I know he won't take any offense if I do.

"I mean, I knew you guys had a lot of stuff with all the loaded moving trucks, but I didn't realize it'd nearly all go in your room." I snicker and point to the various items hanging from his ceiling. The room is massive, three times the size of my own across the street. It's filled with diagrams, models, and in-depth architectural sketches. I'm convinced he's a legit genius and he's only humoring me when it comes to studying.

Axel snorts, rolling over on to his back to watch me. I keep poking and lifting various items and then shooting him a raised brow or wide eyes to exaggerate my point. He's been busy asking me questions for a review I have on an upcoming test this Friday. He's seriously the best study partner, always trying to keep me on track. I never understood why teachers leave tests for the end of the week. I feel like it's their one small victory to make us sweat over the weekend about a potential failing grade.

"Stop slacking, Lois Lane, and get your inquisitive mind where it should be."

"Mm? And where is that exactly?" I tap my chin, grinning playfully. "I'm sure you have an answer for that as well?"

"Yes, indeed, I do. It should be right here…on this bed," he declares, and my breath catches.

Axel has no idea how many times that exact bed he's referring to has been the center of my attention and daydreams. He's always lying there or sitting in his desk chair, completely alluring without having the slightest idea about it. When he peels his uniform shirt off after school and stretches out like he usually does in front of me, I find myself having difficulty breathing. Also thinking of anything other than him and how inviting that bed looks, for that matter. School work be damned…the reason I've needed all the extra help I can get is because my brain turns to mush when it comes to any of the quads being near me.

Attempting to keep the mood lighthearted, I skip closer, making him chuckle and roll his eyes at my playfulness. Axel's always so serious that I love making him smile and laugh, even if it's at my expense acting like a dork sometimes. Plopping down beside him, I lie on my side facing his long form. He reminds me of a cat, but a powerful one like a cougar or a panther all stretched out watching it's dinner, trying to decide if it's hungry enough to move from its comfy spot.

"Mm...and what interesting things would I find in your room if we decided to study over there instead?"

Screwing up my nose, my heart beats quicker from being so close to his body and a bed. I respond a bit breathily, "Just an unfortunate amount of pink everywhere, nothing worth seeing."

"Nah, I can definitely see you as a pink girl, and there's nothing wrong with that." The pad of his pointer finger tenderly trails over my jawline, making me shiver with a delightful bout of telltale chills. He does this sometimes when I'm least expecting it, touching me sweetly and making me crave more than I should with him.

"Ugh, let me guess, it's the hair, isn't it? Purple hair, so I'm automatically thrust into the girly girl category. I don't *not* like the color pink; it's just not my most favorite."

"Oh, and what is?"

Biting my lip, I curl my toes as I admit, "Dove gray." I've discovered it's the color of Axel's irises when he's thinking about something hard enough. He has a brilliant mind. It's one of the things I like most about him, along with how kind and patient he is with me.

He stares intently into my eyes before moving his hands to cup my cheeks with his palms. They aren't rough like Tristan's, but not completely soft either. He has a balance. His thumbs lightly rub over the hollow of my cheeks and my lips part with pleasant surprise. He's never gone this far with touching me before; it's usually a single fingertip or wrapping me in a sweet hug.

His name leaves me on a sigh, "Axel." Upon hearing it like that, he leans in. His tender, careful lips barely brush against mine, releasing a shaky breath with the soft caress. My body stills with the touch, not wanting to jostle him out of the passionate spell. He's not remotely finished, however, as with the next move of his mouth, he draws my lips in between his to gently suck.

"Mmm." I release a quiet moan at the feeling his mouth inflicts. My body hums with the desire to wrap my arms around him tightly, and for him to press his body closer against mine.

He answers my verbal need with a returning groan as his tongue enters my mouth. He takes a tentative stroke against my tongue and then thrusts for more. Axel's movements are slow and purposeful, drawing me out from under my shell in search of more. With the excited joining of our eager mouths, his hands slide into my hair. His fingers wind into my soft lavender locks, his grip tight but not too painful that it's uncomfortable. Axel seems to be feeling this as much as I am and it's a beautiful thing to feel wanted in return by a boy you can't seem to get enough of.

There's a loud, quick knock on his door interspersed with a short, gruff, "Bro?" Brent calls through the thick oak barrier. His low, gravelly tone has me jerking back so quickly, I fall onto the floor trying to escape Axel's touch before we're discovered crossing that line of friendship and something more. My cheeks light with fire, embarrassment and shock quickly taking over. But not only that, I'm supposed to marry his brother, for heaven's sake. Yet here I lie, secretly thrilled about making out with Axel while Tristan could be right down the damn hall! The worst part of all is that I can't even make myself not like what just happened between us. I loved every minute of it, no matter my conscious screaming at me that it was wrong, and I should feel some type of way.

Axel swallows and then clears his throat. He pushes his glasses up as they're slanted crookedly across his cheek and yells out a disheveled, "Yeah?" His voice is gruff, sounding more like Brent's in the moment. He must've been as enthralled with our kiss as I was. That thought offers me a small dose of satisfaction inside knowing I'm not the only one.

The door opens with Brent poking his head in—short, closely-cropped hair making its appearance first. He takes in the scene before him, the indentions on the bed from our bodies, my flushed face and awkward placement on the ground, looking ridiculously disheveled. He frowns deeply and opens his mouth, then closes it. Inhaling deeply, as if collecting his thoughts, he finally speaks. "Dad will be back in town in about an hour or so. He wants us to have dinner together."

Patting down any stray lavender strands back in place, I stand. Wanting to make the discomfort disappear, I mumble, "I should get going. Thanks for your help, Axel."

Brent snorts, rudely interrupting. "That's my brother, always willing to help out."

Swallowing, I dart a look at Axel through my lashes, but he's too busy glaring at Brent. "I'll see you guys at school," I reply and close the flap of my messenger bag then position the wide strap in place over my shoulder.

Brent's intimidating, cerulean stare halts me in place as he rasps, "I'm sure our daddy dearest will want Tristan's future wife to be in attendance. Problem with that?"

With a silent shake of my head, I add, "I'll go change into something more appropriate."

He grunts, not saying anything to me in return but pins his moody brashness back on Axel. "Also, you may want to clean the lip gloss off your lips, Ax. Sparkles aren't your best look."

Axel huffs, getting to his feet and I manage to escape by Brent's hulking form before anything else comes of it. I'm down the hall a few paces when I hear their deep voices rise in conflict. I'm able to catch Axel telling his older brother to mind his business, and it has me rattled. The real confusing part though is when Brent reminds Axel that I belong to all the de Lacharrieres not only him and demands he share.

I can't help but wonder what Tristan would say if he were to hear them. He's come off as possessive toward me so far, and the thought of him catching Brent meeting me in the girl's locker room or Axel kissing me has me a bit on edge. I don't want to hurt any of them, and it gets harder each day when I find myself looking for their faces above all others. One thing's for sure, I need the perfect dress for dinner. I have to keep Tristan distracted from the newfound edginess between his two brothers.

I'm just about to dip into the girl's restroom to take off my hunter green academy-issued sweater when my name rings out through the hallway's loud speakers to report to the front office. There's no time for me to worry about my name being scribbled on the restroom door. In bright metallic sharpie, it says how I'll give free blow jobs to any boys who enter and bring a twenty-dollar bill. It's demeaning in the sexual sense and also by making me appear inferior to my peers. Devon is richer than me, but I'm not hurting for cash, and amongst the rich, it's a pretty nasty dig. She's a bitch, and no matter how I react to her, it doesn't change.

I've been a bit nervous lately since the other girls around the school besides Devon have upped their tormenting. There are females glaring at me around every corner along with it being the same way in each of my classes. The real kicker is that I've never spoken to half of them before and they've decided they hate me, all because of Devon's newfound negative attitude around me. The boys keep me on my toes enough without adding in extras to worry about. So not only do I have to deal with rude people, but the anxiety of four insanely gorgeous, temperamental guys is making me sweat more, and I keep feeling overheated on a daily base.

There's not much I can do about any of the girls taunting and ugly remarks either. I could attempt to report them to the front office or to my teachers, but with so many students involved now, it would be nearly impossible to get any kind of favorable outcome. I'm kicking myself for not reporting them when it first started.

I foolishly believed if I ignored them all that it would stop and they'd eventually leave me alone. That's not the case, though. Now it's me against nearly every other girl in the school. Even if Sam was right about the girls wanting to be like me before, I doubt they'd want to be me now. I just wish I knew what changed so swiftly so I could try to fix it and regress back to my unexciting routine.

Veering away from the bathroom and the door's offensive remarks, I make my way into the office. "Hi, I was paged over the intercom," I greet the lady at the front desk. She's in the academy's standard edition staff uniform which consists of black slacks and polo top. The classroom instructors wear suits as does any of the upper faculty, but all other school employees have the polos and pants. It makes it easier to dissect who is who around here for visitors and new students.

"Yes, thank you, Kresley. Please head down the hall and to the left. The guidance counselor was requesting your presence in her office."

"Okay," I reply, surprised. The only time I see a counselor is when I need to discuss my schedule. Could one of my teachers have complained about my grades or asked for me to be transferred out? I thought with all the studying I've been doing that my grades were perfectly fine.

Coming to a stop at the first door down the dimly-lit office hallway, I lightly knock on the door. It swings open immediately with a pensive looking Mrs. Shoemaker. She's got her phone in one hand and a school issued walkie-talkie in the other. I've seen the custodians wearing and using them to communicate spills and such.

"Kresley," she sighs. "Thank you for getting here quickly. We need to discuss an issue before it draws any more attention and parents start calling us."

"Sure, am I, um, in trouble or something?"

"No, but please follow me out to the student parking lot."

"Okay." I fall into step behind her, wondering what on earth this could be about. Maybe they're relining the parking area? But that couldn't be it; they do all that kind of stuff during summer and the other shorter breaks. The only other thing I can come up with is if they were mowing and my car was scratched, though that is usually on the weekends, so I'm pretty much at a loss on what to think.

Silently, I follow her down the school hall and out the double doors. We take the steps leading onto the sidewalk, and my curiosity only increases with each stride as to why we need to have this conversation or whatever it is outside, instead of in her comfortable office. My mouth slackens in shock when we reach the lot, and it registers. A devastated gasp escapes from my open mouth as my eyes adjust to the bright sunshine, and I can see my car clearer. My precious Jaguar has been vandalized, the navy paint no longer gleaming with wax. I'm scared to think of what the white leather inside must look like as well. The tinted windows are busted out, and there are glass shards all over the surrounding pavement.

"Oh, my God!" I shriek and take off in a sprint to get closer and see the extent of damage. Down the side, scraped severely into the custom dark blue paint is the word WHORE. It appears that someone took a large chunk of the broken glass and carved deeply through the multiple layers of paint, reaching the metal underneath.

I don't have any idea whatsoever to say about it except, how could someone hate me so much to do this?

Chapter Eight

I'm far too emotionally distracted by the destruction of my car to notice Cole step up behind me. The counselor, Mrs. Shoemaker, gestures to him, making his presence known. She shares, "Thanks to Mr. de Lacharriere for reporting this vandalism incident to the office. Otherwise, it may have sat out here until school let out. We'd have been forced to revoke your parking permit, unfortunately, due to the dangerous state of your vehicle."

She's too concerned about it reflecting poorly on the school that there's no compassion or empathy offered to me. I'm just another spoiled rich kid, right? Wrong. My father will be absolutely furious. I have no idea how I can possibly breach the subject and tell my parents about this without a violent outcome. It wasn't my fault, yet I know I'll take the full blame for it and be punished.

Turning my body away, so my back faces the school, I break into sobs. It's just a stupid car, but at the same time, it's not at all. This was my sweet sixteen birthday gift from my parents, but that doesn't matter. What does matter is the punishment I'll be facing because of someone's malicious idea of entertaining torment to inflict upon me. They may've seen me upset in the halls from the taunting, but I refuse to allow anyone who may be eagerly watching from the academy witness me so distraught. If I do, it'll be giving them the exact response they wanted, I suppose.

"Shhh beba," Cole soothes, coming to wrap me in his strong arms. He's smaller than Tristan and Brent muscle wise, but he's still solid, and his embrace is everything in the moment. I secretly consider him to be a bit of a dick, but his comforting warmth is much appreciated right now. I need to lean on someone else's strength because mine has depleted with all my stress and worry.

Mrs. Shoemaker doesn't comment on Cole hugging me but does say, "You'll need to take care of this mess straightaway, Kresley. Like I mentioned, you're fortunate Cole brought this to our attention before others saw it, so you have a little bit of time to fix this mess. Harvard Academics won't hesitate to withdraw your parking pass and notify your parents before the end of the day. I'd hate to see that happen to you due to something you had no control over."

Cringing, I bury my head into Cole's chest as I tense with the added stress of her words. I don't know how to fix any of this. I'm freaking out for several reasons, and she's worried about me grabbing a broom or whatever. Someone despises me so much they'd vandalize my car; I have this huge mess to clean up before classes let out shortly, and my parents will be positively livid. The only person acting like they give two shits is Cole freaking de Lacharriere, and it has my head spinning. Maybe he's being kind for Tristan's sake? Who knows.

Cole grumbles, his chest vibrating as he replies, "I've taken care of it, Mrs. Shoemaker. If you'll leave us to it, I'll make sure this mess is cleaned up and Kresley makes it home safely. Oh, and if the headmaster has any concerns, he's welcome to call my father."

"Yes, of course. That's very admirable of you," the counselor notes before walking off. Cole could be a serial killer, but no one would question him, as his daddy's now the wealthiest contributor to our little slice of prep school. Cole's the Harvard Academy's Elite, the untouchable, where the staff is concerned.

My nose runs with my hysterics, and I sniff a few times, begging myself not to make me look even worse. Red-rimmed eyes, tear-streaked cheeks, and puffy skin is plenty as far as I'm concerned. "What did you mean when you said you took care of it?" I hiccup with a tearful sob.

"Shh, shh mon belle. Calm down," he hums as a mammoth of a tow truck pulls into the lot right in front of my banged-up Jaguar.

"It's being towed?"

He nods. "And I have a roadside crew coming to clean up all the glass as well. The lot will be back to new when everyone leaves class and comes outside. They'll never know it happened and the school won't be able to penalize you either."

"Wow..." Sighing, my head tilts back some so I can gaze up at him. Cole stepping in and taking care of this stressful situation for me was not something I'd ever expect from a de Lacharriere. "Thank you. I wouldn't have known where to start," I admit softly, sincere with genuine gratitude. Now, I have to break the news to Dad and prepare for his reaction.

"Mm," his chest rumbles at my gratefulness.

He gestures to the Jaguar as the tow truck driver approaches. Cole uses one hand to scribble a quick signature while keeping me safe and secure with his other arm. He hands the man a crisp new one-hundred-dollar bill before the guy walks away to start loading my car up on the trailer.

Cole gives me a squeeze and mumbles, "So calm down now, yeah?"

Another hiccup escapes me as a fresh round of tears crests and falls unceremoniously. "I appreciate it, really. I'm just pretty much freaking out over not having a car now. I know insurance will make sure a shop fixes the paint and the windows, but what if it happens again? And what in the hell do I tell my parents? Oh,

God..." I cry, wanting to turn in and just crumble.

"I know a guy," he soothes, leading me toward his sleek Aston Martin Vanquish. "I called him when I discovered your vehicle was ruined. He's the one who set up the tow and cleanup for us, but that's not all I asked him for."

Regarding him curiously, I wait for him to continue. Rather than speak about it anymore, he opens the passenger door of his vehicle and beckons for me to climb into the obsidian convertible. This thing is fast; I don't have to ride in it to know. With Cole as the owner, I'd bet good money he likes to race it. He strikes me as laid-back, but dangerous and a bit reckless as well. So why am I climbing into a car with him? Because at this point, why the fuck not? I'm already going to be in serious trouble, may as well follow this rabbit hole wherever it ends up leading me.

The drive passes by quickly, and I'm surprised when Cole brings us to his house, directly across the street from my own. Not that my parents would notice me over here anyhow. The house is too far off from the road that they can't tell who's coming and going in the neighborhood unless they're pulling out of the driveway. It just wasn't where I was expecting him to bring us; I figured we'd be heading to the tow shop or a collision place to discuss how to fix the car.

Cole takes his time driving down the paved path leading to the quads' immaculate home. He eventually slows and pulls to a stop right beside a brand-new cherry red sports car that gleams in the sunlight. He holds a hand up, basically telling me to be patient and wait. I do as he instructs and watch as he comes around to open my door. He may be dickish most of the time at school, but someone obviously taught him some manners. As soon as the door's open, I'm freeing myself from the seat belt and climbing out.

I stride toward the front door, but I don't make it too far before Cole snatches my wrist. Twisting me back around toward him, I trip over my feet and fall right into his strong, waiting embrace. I'd like to believe it's my poor balance, but he seems to have me right where he wanted. I can feel his intense scrutiny as he stares down at me. There's so much tension building between us suddenly that I can't seem to meet his gaze. Instead, I concentrate on his nose—it's a bit pointy. He truly strikes me as an aristocrat. His regal French heritage is easily worn on his features, and gosh, does it make him handsome. "Over here," he quietly rasps the demand, and my nipples tighten in response. Thankfully, he can't see them through my thick academy shirt, or he'd quickly discover how my body responded to his raspy orders.

Swallowing down the feeling as much as possible, I lick my lips and nod. Cole leads me to the other side of the new car. It's so glossy, and it reminds me of a ruby. He waves his free hand in the direction of the sporty number. "It's yours, beba."

My eyes light up as I take it in with more detail. "You're letting me borrow a car?" I ask innocently, and he chuckles, amused. It's not a pleasant laugh, either. The sound reminds me more of the big bad wolf, rather than the boy beside me with a sweet gesture.

"Nah, I bought it for you."

"You bought me a Porsche?" I nearly stammer with a gasp. "But...why? Why would you waste any of your money on me?"

"So you would be in debt to me," he admits with a nonchalant shrug, and my nose scrunches. The guy before me is more confusing than any of the other guys I've met in the past—as are his three brothers. They're all so back-and-forth and moody. It makes me think they're playing some sort of twisted game with me. If that were the case, I'd be able to figure it out, right? I can't think about the possibilities of that being accurate when I have so much going on right now.

"What could I possibly have that you'd want?"

"This." He grins wickedly and tucks his hand behind my neck. Drawing me forward into his chest again, his head dips, and he claims my mouth. Sensations explode through my limbs—first, he's comforting me, then fixing my problem, and now, I'm surrounded in his taste and his tender mouth. His kiss is nothing like

Tristan's or Axel's. Cole's lips on mine are everything I wasn't expecting and everything I didn't realize I wanted. He's been hiding this other side of him from me, and he's utterly amazing. I'm thrown off-kilter trying to wrap my mind about who Cole really is when his walls drop and he allows you in.

His tongue plays with mine, the movements making me moan with desire. Cole catches it with his mouth, kissing the sounds away. His lips are soft, the movements tender in their pursuit, yet demanding. He's not taking no for an answer from me, that's for sure. Not that I'd tell him no. I wouldn't stand a chance if I did, so why bother fighting it?

The sexy Cajun can't possibly be oblivious to everyone's stares, mine included. I try to look away, but even I catch myself silently panting after one or more of the four of them. And now I've kissed not only one of Tristan's brothers but two. I can't possibly worry over it at the moment, as Cole surrounds me, beckoning my full attention.

My fingers wind through his short, messily-styled hair. The cropped locks are soft and the perfect length for me to tug on them a bit. His free hand snakes around my waste until it rests just above my butt. My mind silently chants for him to grab it and I'm kind of freaking out that I want him to touch me all over so badly. At least let me act appalled while I'm really secretly flattered to have the bad boy's attention. It's his deep Southern drawl, his warm embrace, and the heady scent of his cologne that sort of swallows me up and has my knees shaking. He may be a dick most days, but today, he's a dick who's a damn good kisser, and he smells delicious.

Breaking away, he leans his forehead on mine, gazing into my irises. "It was worth the wait, beba. Yeah?" His husky drawl has deepened from the intimate moment we just finished sharing, and the lowered tone has the same effect on me as eating a hot fudge sundae.

I couldn't agree more, not that I can voice it aloud right now or ever. The rock on my finger weighs heavily on my hand and my mind. "But Tristan..." I start to say, and he shakes his head, quieting me.

"Tristan is grown; he knows that if I wanna kiss you, I will. The same goes for any of my brothers."

"Any of them?" I echo on a breath, and his lips turn up, amused with my reaction.

"Mm. Only de Lacharrieres, shorty. Any others will be dealt with by the quad." It's incredible how even threats leaving his mouth can sound so deliciously enticing. It's that Southern accent; for some reason, it's always much more pronounced with him than with the others. Listening to him call me *'beaba'* and *shortaay'* reminds me of thick, gooey, sugary maple syrup. His voice gives me crazy good goosebumps all over.

I keep my thoughts to myself, and after a moment, Cole releases my hand, placing the key pod to the Porsche in its place. His chin tilts, and he nods across the street toward my house. "Go take you a long bath and relax," he orders, and I smile at his thoughtfulness. Cole's usually a jerk, so it's not at all what I was expecting from him. This entire day has thrown me for a loop.

"That actually sounds like a really wonderful idea."

My palm's sweaty around the key pod as excitement fills my chest over my new car, along with memories from his lips. I can't wait to drive this beauty, even if it's only down my driveway for now. "Thank you for this." I flail my empty hand at the car. "And, well, for everything today. I would've been lost without you stepping in to help." I press a kiss to his cheek. My gratitude and the kiss is nothing in comparison, but it's completely genuine, and the only way I can offer him my thanks.

Cole flashes a sexy grin and opens the driver side door for me. I climb in, sending him an appreciative smile. "Tomorrow, beba," he promises and closes the door, and I can't help but hope that he really does show up tomorrow at school. Thoughtful Cole is definitely someone I would like to be around, especially with how broody Brent and Tristan usually tend to be.

The car drives like a dream and has that new car and leather smell that makes me giddy inside. I almost take it for a spin around the neighborhood, but decide to take Cole's suggestion to heart and go straight home to soak in a tub full of steaming hot water and bubbles. I don't get the chance to make it there, however, because Dad's home early from work or golfing or whatever he does during the day.

I'm barely through the door, with my foot on the first step toward freedom and he beckons me. His voice carries from his office down the hall that's tucked behind the massive staircase off to the right. You'd never know there was a hallway there unless it's pointed out. The architect designed it, so it looks like a decorative bump out at first glance and not a gloomy hall.

"Hey, Daddy." I paste a smile on my face as I breeze through his doorway, attempting to keep the mood in the room light. I need to butter him up somehow before he finds out about my car and loses his temper. So I do what any teenager would and stall. Not only that, but I also remain a good fifteen feet away from him. He's thrown things in the past, so keeping distance in a potential disaster conversation with him is smart.

"Come here." His brows rise, his gaze watching me closely. He knows what I'm doing by standing back, and he's not having it. This could turn bad in the blink of an eye.

"Yes sir," I respond and step farther into the room. I stop behind one of the tall chairs in front of his desk, though. I'm not stupid; I know to always try and keep something in front of me.

"Closer," he demands and moves his chair back a bit and points to the spot directly next to him.

Swallowing my fear down, I draw on any courage I have remaining and pray for him to be in a decent mood. With a deep calming breath, I shuffle around the oversized chair, then move to the side of the desk and stop exactly on the spot where he'd pointed. I keep my eyes trained on the floor, silently pleading he doesn't strike my face for my car being ruined.

"I checked the cameras when I received the gate alert that your code was punched in. You're home a bit early, hm?"

My bottom lip trembles as I whisper a shaky, "Yes sir, I am."

"Look at me," he demands. My hands clench into fists to keep them from quivering, and I hide them behind my back as I lift my eyes to meet his calculating gaze. "Whose car were you driving when you pulled in?"

"Mine."

"Oh?" He clicks his tongue, and coolly asks, "Did I give you permission to buy another?"

This is *so* bad. He's far too calm that it has my stomach twisting with nausea. I hope I don't puke on his carpet; it'll only infuriate him further. "N-no, sir. It was a gift."

His fingers tap on his desk as his head tilts. He looks me over. "A gift...from whom...the de Lacharrieres?"

I nod. "Someone, um, th-they scratched the Jaguar at school. I had just found out about it when they had the car towed and replaced." Fear curdles in my stomach, my body tensing as I wait for him to explode at the news. It takes everything in me not to jump back to the chair and cower behind it for some sense of safety.

My father's chuckle has me shaking my head with shock. My mouth pops open as I gawk, not used to seeing him happy like this in the middle of the day. He chortles, reaching out to clasp my shoulder affectionately. Pride shines in his eyes as he boasts, "My girl! You've managed to snag the richest boy in school. He gives you a big diamond and asks to marry you, and now shortly after he's already bought you a hundred-thousand-dollar sports car before you've exchanged vows or had a proper holiday!" He laughs again. "I was worried, but hell, you've made me proud."

Licking my lips, I flash a timid smile. "Thank you." Though I've done nothing, in reality, it's been the boys, not me. I really don't know how I should be reacting to him like this. I was anticipating him putting me through the ringer and having to hide bruises from my peers at school. There's no way I can let him find out that Tristan's brothers have kissed and flirted with me too.

"In fact, I have something just for this," he sniggers and digs through one of the bottom desk drawers. He pulls out a black velvet box. "I had this saved, but you deserve to have it." Popping the top open a sparkly platinum diamond tennis bracelet shines back at me.

"It's beautiful," I whisper with my throat still dry and croaky.

He beams in return. "Wear it tomorrow. It'll make that boy jealous wondering who bought it for you, and I'll bet he'll be sending a bigger one over to take its place on your wrist."

I hold my hand out and watch anxiously as he clasps the sparkling bracelet on my wrist. I don't want to make anyone jealous, especially not Tristan, but my father obviously thinks it's a good idea. He may enjoy playing games, but I don't. I'm already dealing with enough at school as it is without adding in any more drama.

"Although, your mother tells me he's already sent multiple boxes of gifts for you."

I nod, and explain, "Yes. Tristan had some fine chocolates and hand stitched undergarments imported from France."

"You'll wear them for him, but don't eat the chocolate," he demands. "I won't have you getting fat and lazy before he signs the marriage license."

I cringe, but thankfully, he misses it. "Okay."

He squeezes my shoulder once more and gives it a little shake. "Keep it up, honey." With that parting remark, he dismisses me, and I practically run to the safety of my room.

I need that scholarship more than ever. I have to get the fuck out of here and away from my future being planned for me. I have to be far from my crazy father and the off chance that this engagement could fall through. Lord knows if that happens, my life will be ruined for sure.

My phone rings and a sense of relief washes over me at finally seeing Brandon's name flashing across the screen. He hasn't spoken to me since Tristan had me start sitting with him at lunch and flashed my engagement ring to the entire cafeteria. Brandon's been avoiding and tiptoeing around me like a kicked dog. After the fifth time I called him to explain and he let it go to voicemail, I backed off realizing he wasn't accidentally missing my call but doing it on purpose.

Of course, my feelings were hurt at him blowing me off, but at the same time, I understand why he's keeping his distance. I think he's in self-preservation mode, or at least, he has been. He's never been quiet about his feelings for me and how he wants us to be more than friends. I've always had him in the friend zone, regardless of his resiliency. Not having him around lately has felt like a piece of me has been missing and I don't like it. I broke down and asked Sam if he hates me, but she swears he doesn't. However, she did say that I've broken his heart and that sucks. It makes me feel like crap because I really do care about him, just not in the same way he does about me.

Boys should altogether be on the back burner for me. I need to be focused on getting accepted to a college. And not only the admission process but also be awarded a fully-paid scholarship. It'll be tough enough to work to support myself and handle the full school load, let alone pay for college courses. I don't want to depend on my father for anything, and once I'm gone, I don't plan on falling back on my parents for assistance. Everything with that would come with strings attached, and that's what I'm trying so hard to escape from.

Yet, I can't seem to help but find myself smitten with the quadruplets. Tristan drives me crazy being bossy. Brent is pensive and usually keeps to himself. Cole is an asshole who is also surprisingly thoughtful, and Axel is easily sliding into the best friend spot next to Sam. If Brandon and I can't work through his hurt feelings and wounded pride, then I could easily see Axel filling his place. It makes me sad because I've known Brandon most of my life, but it is what it is, I guess.

It doesn't help that they're all insanely gorgeous, cocky, and at times even flirt with me. I've been kissed by three of them, and Brent was an almost kiss that still has me furtively wishing he'd have just gone for it and given in to temptation. At times I can't stand the four jerks that somehow have begun to rule the academy, yet I can't seem to get through my days without them being included in some way either. It doesn't help that nearly every girl in school wants them and I'm wearing an engagement ring from the charismatic one who also happens to be the family football dream come true. It's unwillingly morphed me into public enemy number one in their books. If only I could come out and tell them all that I don't want the damn diamond, that I'd rather have my freedom versus the boy.

With a relieved breath, I hit accept and say, "Brandon." A sigh of relief escapes me that he's speaking to me again. It's our longest stint of time not conversing with each other.

"Jesus Kresley, you okay? I just found out about what happened to your car. The academy was ripe with gossip at the end of the day, but I didn't know the rumor held any merit until Sam cornered me about it at practice."

My heart fills, my chest warming at the sound of his voice and knowing he still cares about my well-being. "I'm okay…a bit shaken up if I'm being honest about it."

"Fuck, I bet. I still can't believe anyone had the guts to take it that far. I'm glad you weren't around or who knows what the psycho could've done to you as well. You want me to come over, so you're not alone when you have to tell your father?"

I don't air what happens out in the open, but being friends with Brandon and Sam throughout the years they've managed to catch bits and pieces. They don't know just how explosive my dad can be, but I'm sure they have their own ideas of what kind of monster he is. They probably aren't too far off either. Brandon's father can be pretty controlling and cruel at times; unfortunately, for my friend, his dad doesn't hide it as well from the public as mine has managed to so far. The entire school has witnessed his dad lose it on him after a football game gone bad before. Sam and I were crying watching him treat Brandon so horribly, but we couldn't do anything about it. The school staff eventually stepped in to soften it from coming back on the academy. Otherwise, Sam and I could only try to comfort Brandon. He was mortified, of course, and wouldn't speak to anyone for an entire week.

"Thank you, but he was already here at home when I arrived. Since I was back early as well, I had to explain what happened to my car as soon as I walked in the door."

"Oh wow," he says, a different degree of concern and compassion coating his voice. "And you're okay...right? Do you need me to come get you or bring you anything? I'll be there, just say the word and no one will keep me out of that house."

Tears crest at his thoughtfulness and because I know telling him the rest, about Cole helping me and being rewarded with the tennis bracelet will only hurt him. That's definitely not what I want. I wish I could have him come over so we could talk in person and I could try to let him down less than just outright saying it over the phone. Before, it would've been fine to invite him here as long as I gave my mom some notice; you know, for her to keep up appearances and all. Now, however, it can't happen. If I invite another boy over that isn't Tristan or his brothers, no matter how good a friend, the length of time I've known them or me swearing it's strictly platonic, it would be a deal breaker for my father. His good mood would vanish almost instantly, and I'd be punished for what he'd assume would be me putting my arrangement with Tristan in jeopardy.

"I wish you could come over; I feel like I haven't gotten to spend time with you in forever."

"I can leave right now and be on my way," he replies immediately.

"I-uh...I'm sorry, but it's just not a good time."

"Did he *hurt* you, Kresley?" Brandon's voice turns angry, and anxiety grows that he won't listen to me, and he'll show up here. Wincing, I shake my head but realize he can't see me. I'm used to video chatting with Sam. I'm glad we're not able to see each other, or he'd know I was holding back some details from him. He's always been good at reading me.

"No-no, nothing like that. He was actually pretty okay about everything."

"Wow," he remarks. "I almost can't believe it. I've seen you upset and worried for much smaller reasons before. I'm glad, though. Maybe he's finally realizing he shouldn't scare you like he has in the past. You're the smart one, Kres; you'll be off to college in no time, just wait and see."

Biting my lip, I sigh, "Thanks, Brandon, but I won't hold my breath." I don't like admitting it, but it's true. My father won't ever change, and I'd be a fool to believe otherwise. "I did get a new car, so that's the good news. I hope no one messes with it again; I don't know what I'll do."

"Who the hell would do that to you?" he asks with resentment lacing the question.

"I have no idea, trust me. I was completely caught off guard to see that someone hates me so much."

"They're fucking idiots. No one has any reason to dislike you or be mean to you. Fuck them all."

"Thanks, Brandon." I smile to myself at his proclamation. "I've missed this. I've missed you."

"I needed some time."

"I understand. I hope you know that you'll always be my friend, Brandon."

He huffs. "A friend. Yeah. I gotta go, Kres, just wanted to make sure you didn't need me."

The way he says it makes my fist squeeze in frustration. He wants me to need him, and I do, just not the way he wishes. I miss having my goofy, easygoing friend around, especially with how malicious the girls have been to me at the academy lately. I haven't necessarily hated school in the past; if anything, it's been an escape for me as I've gotten older. This year just sucks. I feel sorry for people who have to experience bullying—their entire time in school has to be complete hell. I kind of understand why some kids go as far as committing suicide or run away. No one should experience such hatred, especially without some sort of an escape away from it.

"I'll see you tomorrow?" I probe, hopeful. I'm not looking forward to telling him about my car, but I hope he'll at least talk to me about other stuff. His silent treatment has gone on for too long.

"Yep, and if I see any of those assholes treating you wrongly, I'm putting them in the fucking trash cans. Give the fucks a taste of their own treatment."

A giggle bursts free at the image of Brandon picking up random rude kids and tossing them in the school trash cans. I shouldn't laugh about something like that, but I do anyway.

He whispers, "There she is. I missed that sound."

My laugh catches in my throat, and I quickly say, "See you tomorrow, Brandon."

"Bye, beautiful," he murmurs, and I end the call.

It's so good to talk to him, but he's still calling me beautiful, and the last thing I want is Tristan or Brent hearing it. The fight following that comment would break my heart. Boys shouldn't make you choose, yet they always seem to. How do I pick between my best friends and the guys I can't seem to get out of my head? How am I supposed to choose one guy, when I'm quickly becoming attached to all four of them?

Chapter Nine

The following weeks are basically the same miserable routine of harassment, minus my car being destroyed again. The mistreatment continues, the girls getting ballsier as the days go by. I've never been a fighter, and I haven't had to stand up for myself much in the past, so I'm stuck with a lost feeling. I'm a naturally kind person. I firmly believe that kindness is free, so being bitchy back to the mean girls is a struggle for me, especially when it's all day every day. When someone's rude, I stop from immediately responding and try to think first that maybe they're having a bad day or something's going on in their life that has made them act that particular way. However, when it's the same girls being uncouth day in and day out, it's hard to not strike back. Sam, on the other hand, has no issue being a bitch right back, and her middle fingers have become her favorite response.

Most of these girls I've been around most of my life, and they've always been reasonably kind to me, or they didn't really speak to me. Now, it's like I'm a scuffed-up pair of Louboutin's you find on the sale rack. The kind you occasionally try on but then chuck to the back of the closet rather than wear or donate them.

"Has he invited you to homecoming yet?" Sam inquires randomly as we head for class.

The halls are decorated in various school spirit gear. Homecoming will be here quickly, and while it's nothing I've paid much attention to in the past, aside from attending the game, our school makes a huge deal out of it the entire week prior. There's an exclusive newsletter about it, morning announcements featuring various football players, nominations, and bake sale with themed concessions, a door decorating contest, prizes, pep rally, spirit day, court voting, the football game, a dance, and the crowning ceremony. I'm sure I'm forgetting something, but it's a bit over the top. Not surprising, though, as a few previous football players from here have gone off to play pro.

"No," I shake my head and sip from my bottled cucumber and strawberry infused water. "But he's probably focused on the game anyway. Tristan and Brent both will be starting and playing the entire game. You and I both know they're the best players out of the green and blue teams besides Brandon." Rather than the academy's coaches calling the teams A and B, they opted for colors as to not offend any parents and risk losing out on enrollment and athletic fees. I had no idea what any of it meant, but Brandon and Sam explained it all to me.

She claps her hands excitedly, beaming a loaded smile. She's got some idea cooking up; I can read it on her. I doubt it'll be anything I want to take part in as she's always up to something.

"What?" I ask with a groan and end up laughing at her. No matter what crazy ideas she comes up with, I have to at least hear her out. She's my best friend, but she's full of mischief at times.

"I was interviewing coach about the upcoming game, and I overheard your *beau*."

Rolling my eyes, I switch my art issued sketch book and purse to my other hand. "We're not in some classic fairy tale you dork. Besides, he's not my beau, just my fiancé."

We come to a standstill outside my art class. It's one of the few classes I'm not very good at but enjoy it anyhow. I like it because I don't have to overthink when I'm busy creating something. The course has become my in-school sanctuary that I had no idea I'd need so badly this year. It also doesn't hurt that the instructor is friendly and easygoing; most of my other professors are uptight.

Sam leans in, pulling my elbow so we're close enough that people can't easily overhear us. She stage whispers, "Tristan and Brent were talking to Hazel Jacobs."

My brow scrunches, picturing the perfect head varsity cheerleader. I mean, of course, they would talk to her at some point, both guys are varsity football players, and she cheers them on. Jealousy swirls inside my veins, yet I can't bring myself to say anything hateful. I've spoken to Hazel in the past; she's one of the few cheerleaders that's not full of bullshit and glitter. She's smart, helpful and drop-dead gorgeous. It was no surprise the cheerleaders voted her to lead them. Most everyone in school likes Hazel.

But Brent and Tristan? Tristan's my fiancé. Damn, damn, damn. I shouldn't care, yet I do. What if one of them starts dating her? Do they want her? I have no right to be possessive over the quad, but deep down, I am. I've come to think of them as mine, even if they are dicks half the time I see them. I met them first; I'm around at least one of them all the time...I don't know if I can handle watching them with other girls. There's talk of them being with various females around school—that's no surprise—but to see it? I feel sick just thinking about it.

Sam continues, speaking faster as the bell's about to ring and warn us of tardiness. "Actually, that's the wrong description. They weren't chatting, more like demanding." My brow wrinkles, gut churning at what she's going to say. She finishes, and it's just as bad, but in the opposite direction I was expecting. "They're determined that she recruits you to join the cheer squad."

"What?" I gasp, with my mouth dropping open in stunned disbelief. She has to be kidding.

Sam cackles with glee. "I know! My little jogging, purple-haired, book nerd best friend, engaged to the wealthiest boy in school and now a varsity cheerleader too!"

"No way, Sam," I argue. "Everyone here hates me right now. Are you joking? Please tell me you're just screwing with me." My fingers rub my temples in frustration before muttering, "Damn it, I can't believe he did this. I'm definitely not going to homecoming with him…no way."

"This is Tristan and Brent we're talking about, Kres. They do whatever the hell they want, and if they snap their fingers, it'll happen. Anyway, don't be surprised if Hazel stops to talk to you soon about any of it."

"Sam! I can't do this! The season has already started, plus I don't know how to cheer. I definitely don't know their little chants or whatever they're called. Crap, those girls will have way too many opportunities to torture me."

She snorts. "Pah-leese! Tristan is putting you at the top of the food chain. You'll be right beside him with money and now athletics." She winks, flashes a wide smile and takes off down the hall in the opposite direction toward her class. Sam's newfound information echoes in my head, leaving behind a bad taste in my mouth over what's sure to come.

Sam may consider this whole situation the boys have thrust in my direction is a good thing, but I'm not so sure. Any additional attention pointed toward me, and the girls around here will really despise me. The worst of all with them is that I still have no idea why or what in the hell I did to anyone. I damn sure did not ask for Tristan to put a ginormous ring on my finger. Yet, it happened, and I've caught all of the blame for it. The engagement is the only reason I can come up with behind all their maliciousness.

Sliding into my seat, I make it right in time for the bell to ring. A sigh of relief escapes as I place my belongings on the desk, reassured that I get to zone out for over an hour's time.

"Excuse me, everyone." Mr. Hastings stands in the center of

the class, calling our attention to his upcoming directions.

The room is set up so that we sit in one large circle. There aren't many of us in each period due to the size limitations of the seating arrangement. Inside the circle of our desks is usually a small, round table covered in a solid black tablecloth and whatever item we're currently working on whether it's drawing, painting, or sculpting, so we can see it from every angle. Today, the table is missing, and in its place are three large squares covered in plain white sheets. Everyone quiets immediately, waiting for him to let us in on our next assignment.

"If you remember back to the first week you were in here, you took a packet home discussing our assignments. Your parents had to sign a permission slip that you then returned to me."

Murmurs fill the room with everyone either agreeing or shrugging their shoulders. I remember now that he's mentioned it, but otherwise, I'd forgotten all about my mom signing that paper. I never read it; I figured it was just some sort of generic form with the grading requirements or something. Professors have always sent home similar forms in the past, so I don't pay much attention to them aside from getting them signed.

"Today, you will all understand why it was required, as we begin our sketches of the human body. Now, I must insist you act in a mature manor from here on out. Although I'm confident there won't be any issues. I'm passing a basket around the room. Your cellular devices and tablets must be placed in the basket to sit on my desk. This is nonnegotiable, so don't bother arguing about it." There are a few groans in response, but we follow directions.

Rolling my eyes, I drop my cell in as I pass the basket to my left. It's not like we ever have free time to use them in here anyhow, so the groans are a waste of their breath. Art is literally the entire period, and it requires us to be creative in some aspect. Mr. Hastings likes us to keep everything we're working on until the last possible moment, as he says there is always something to improve on no matter what we may believe.

"It'll behoove you to refrain from immature or lewd comments," he continues. "Anyone not heeding that strong suggestion will be written up immediately and sent to the office, if necessary. This happens to be my most talented art pupil, whom has been gracious enough to volunteer his time to be our muse. Be thankful, as I almost asked my seventy-year-old mother in here instead."

Snickers overtake the quiet room at his mom comment. Stark silence quickly follows as our human model strides out of Mr. Hastings attached office. He's in a Sherpa robe, which he promptly drops as he steps into the center of the room, stopping next to the art instructor. Our model is stark naked, save for a small, thin piece of black material covering his front that's been pinned in place. Leaning back, his muscular buttocks sit against one of the oversized blocks as he finds his comfortable pose. His head lifts and his playful, smoky orbs fall on me as I'm sitting directly in front of him. My cheeks heat, as my entire body fills with desire. Sweat dots my brow, and suddenly, I'm feeling a bit feverish.

He's only clad in the black piece of material and obsidian rimmed glasses...and holy shit, Axel is by far the sexiest boy I've ever seen.

After staring at Axel's flawless, bare form yesterday for an entire class period, I made myself scarce. I didn't study with him per our usual routine after school either. I couldn't get him and his nakedness out of my head, nor deny the overwhelming feelings of wanting to run my hands all over that smooth flesh he had on display. I knew if I showed up to study and we were there alone, I'd make a complete fool of myself. Bad enough that he's kissed me in the past; it's been weighing heavily on me. Now add in me seeing him nearly naked in art class, and it has my hormones running rampant.

I'm strung so tightly; I woke up panting from a far too revealing dream. I'd dreamed that instead of Axel walking out alone in art class that all four of them had been there. They were standing in front of my desk, each only wearing the tiny scrap of fabric. I was devastated waking up to find that I'd imagined the whole thing and they weren't really there on display. I shouldn't think that way of the four of them, and even though I try not to, I can't seem to help myself. I'm drawn to each of them in their own unique way. I don't only think of Tristan like I'm supposed to, but rather dream and crave kissing and touching them all. I have to stop this…I'm marrying Tristan!

Sitting in my usual place at lunch the following day, I gesture to the server and ask for my usual meal. The cafeteria's abuzz with excitement. The halls have been overly decorated in our school's football colors along with posters wishing the individual players good luck, and the class doors are covered in wish boards. It's basically a blank door cover that anyone coming or going can draw and write supportive messages on. Each door is decorated, and at the end of the week, the football team votes for their favorite. It's completely overwhelming; everyone, including the staff, is focused solely on the various rapidly-approaching homecoming activities.

I've also been fairly annoyed, as the academy girls have been gawking since at Tristan and Brent in their team jerseys since this morning. I overheard Brent telling Axel and Cole that the coach wants the players in their jerseys and throughout homecoming to spread school spirit before the pep rally takes place. I certainly enjoy seeing them out of their usual school clothes, but wish I was the only one to witness how well their jeans mold to their muscular frames. I swear, if I hear one more girl talk about how they want to grab their asses, I'm going to poke their damn eyes out.

Tristan leans in, his delicious clean, woodsy scent surrounding the two of us. His minty breath hits me as he says, "I want you to be cheering before homecoming. I want you on the side of the field for my game."

The gulp of water I just sucked from the straw and begun to swallow spews from my mouth as I choke at his words. I start coughing as if I'm drowning from the drink, and Sam, sitting on my other side, pounds on my back. She's a good friend.

"Sip and swallow," she sings and then giggles. "Or maybe it's slurp and swallow?" She laughs more.

Rolling my eyes, my gaze lands back on the bossy man-boy to my side. "That's not how it works," I argue. "The girls who cheer at homecoming are the best, their varsity squad." And besides, that freaking game is only a week away. There's no way in hell I could even remotely learn how to cheer in that time frame.

He shrugs. "Doesn't matter, you're mine. You'll be there to cheer for Brent and me."

Sam shakes with giggles as I scowl. This guy can be infuriating. I don't take to being bossed around well either, by anyone other than my father, and I have no choice when it concerns him. I stay too busy, I guess, to allow anyone else to really have the opportunity. Not these guys, though. They're around me most of the day, so they think it's perfectly fine to order me about like their servant.

Tristan continues. "I went ahead and took the liberty and spoke to Hazel on your behalf. She should be chatting with you about it all soon." He waves it off like it's nothing I should be concerned over like I should just go along with it all like a good little fiancée.

My heart thumps rapidly, my fists clenching and then loosening as I exhale, trying to rein my temper in. I may have to marry this pain in the butt, good-looking boy-man, but it doesn't mean I'm going to sit by and let him bulldoze over me. "Exactly Tristan, that's a l-i-b-e-r-t-y!" I spell the word out for emphasis since he seems to speak cheerleader. "You can't go around making decisions for me like this," I hiss quietly so people won't overhear and gossip even more than they already do.

Brent glowers, and while his dark, pissy expression would easily make a full-grown man cower, I'm not afraid of him. He's protected me before, and at this point, I can't believe he'd hurt me, so I glare right back. It's not like he ever tells me what he wants besides ordering me to stay out of trouble and to stick up for myself. If anything, I'm heeding his prior advice, and he should be patting me on the back for it.

My stubborn fiancé ignores my chastising, rolling forward with the conversation. "Do you have something to wear for the homecoming dance?"

With a shrug, I turn away and offer a smile and a thank you to the server for my plate of steaming hot chicken and rice. Eventually, I admit, "I wasn't planning on going. Sam and I usually go to the game but skip out on the dance and everything else."

"Coach wants us to participate in everything school related, especially with homecoming and the festivities."

Axel leans in, his ashy irises sparkling with laughter behind his Clark Kent glasses. "And by default, that means you, too, sweetie." I wouldn't mind his teasing so much if he was back in that cloth from art class.

My gaze bounces between the four similar faces and find matching expressions. They're all projecting the same look that says, *I'm going and they don't care if I argue.*

Releasing a sigh, I give in, "Okay, fine. I can manage that."

Sam hoots. "Hell yeah, more shopping! This is going to be so much fun."

"You on their side or mine, Sam?" Geez, they have her pegged already. If my best friend were in my shoes, she'd be putty in Tristan's arms. All it'd take with her is the diamond ring and him handing over his credit card.

Her perfectly sculpted brow lifts. "One of these boys is going to win homecoming king. You need to be around to show whichever gold digger that wins queen that the de Lacharrieres belong to you no matter the occasion or the size of crown they wear."

My hands fly to my temples, fingers massaging. I can't believe she just went there, and in front of them, to boot. With a huff, I shake my head, and whisper shout, "They're not mine, Samantha! Don't say that sort of thing out loud; someone can overhear you."

A loud scrape draws my attention away from her as Brent swiftly gets to his feet. His piercing regard silently demands so many things that I can't quite figure out. With a huff, he snarls an intense, "Bullshit!" Then he's storming off, leaving me at a loss for words and the rest of the table stunned in silence.

Chapter Ten

Homecoming week came and went, and surprisingly, I had more fun than I'd had in the past years. However, the quads were crazy to think I'd be a cheerleader in a week, even if it was just to show off for them. No way was I putting myself through that much pressure to learn routines and the choreographed half-time dance. We did find a way to compromise, though, after I threatened them that I'd pretend to be sick the entire week and not participate in anything. Sam brought up the idea of me wearing Tristan and Brent's jersey numbers, so I ended up having a special football jersey made in our team's colors. I wore Tristan's number on the back to face the crowd and Brent's number on the front, paired with a cute, short white skirt. I wore spandex underneath of course, not that I was jumping around or anything, but Brent and Cole went all caveman about me only having panties on underneath.

Hazel ended up helping me figure out a way to be a part of everything without coming off as a hot mess. She showed me how to use the megaphone to help chant cheers and pump everyone up in the stands, not that they actually needed any extra encouragement. The parents and students were yelling loudly, excited to see the team play and secure the academy another win. Of course, I dragged Sam into it with me. There was no way I was putting myself out there without her beside me. She wore Brandon's number on her jersey to stick with the "jersey cheer supporter theme," which made him happy to have his own personal cheer-supporter too.

Surprisingly, Hazel and the cheer squad were super sweet about the whole situation and brought up that they should've thought of the idea long ago. I couldn't believe they embraced the idea, along with Sam and me right away. They don't even act jealous when it comes to the guys and me, and it was a breath of fresh air. So now we're officially part of their group, but only in our jerseys and megaphones for the rest of the season.

Apparently, I've seen far too many mean girl movies because I was seriously expecting some vicious hazing from the squad and that hasn't been the case at all. If anything, they've become friends to Sam and me. I've always known who the cheerleaders are, but now they talk to me often. They even say hi in the hallways and wave if they see me farther away. Having backup in the locker room for PE. has helped with keeping the bitchy girls off my case as well. Once Devon caught wind of me being friends with the most popular girls in school, she backed off. Altogether it was a win, and I feel a bit judgmental and snobbish for writing the squad off so quickly in the past.

My days seem to get busier and busier. They're full of homework and tests and time slips by quickly. November's gone in a blink, along with my willpower where the quads are concerned. I thought I could rebuke them without a thought at the beginning of the year, but I've become more attached to having them in my life. Learning their individual personalities and their many differences, I find myself emotionally invested in each of them.

Maybe marrying into the family won't be so bad after all.

The only issue I find myself fighting with daily is that I still like all four of them. Not in the friendly, big brother way either. They've kissed me in random spots, and I'm growing addicted to their affections. Well, all except for Brent. He's held back from kissing me, even though it's nearly happened dozens of times. I'm to the point that I wish he'd give in. The intensity between us has me on edge. I shouldn't desire him like that when I'm set to marry Tristan. It's *his* ring I wear on my finger.

It's hard to think like that, however, when they're constantly making comments about me belonging to all of them. Does that mean what I think it does? That they can each kiss me, touch me, and be with me whenever they wish? How on earth could that work when Tristan and I are married? Will it all suddenly come to a stop? They may be able to pull that off, but I'm certainly not able too. I don't only like them romantically, though; they're my friends now as well, which makes it especially confusing.

"Father decided it's time we host an engagement party," Tristan mentions randomly once we've come back from Thanksgiving break. We're not like average schools that only get two or three days off; we get an entire week plus both weekends off for Thanksgiving. Most of our families travel and go on vacation or else have people visiting. We spent the holiday eating with Tristan and his family, of course. Their chef prepared a full classic holiday spread, and I swear it was the best Thanksgiving food I've ever tasted. Later that evening, Cole and Axel both took turns smearing my throat with pumpkin pie and whipped cream and licking it off. It'll defiantly be a holiday that I never forget.

Screwing up my nose toward Tristan, I huff out a short laugh, "Why? We've been engaged for months now, and everyone already knows. There were photographers taking photos the very moment you dropped to your knees and slid the ring on my finger.

I think a party and announcement is a bit of a moot point by now, don't you?"

I still believe the engagement and photo op was all premeditated and his father had arranged them there knowing it would make the front page in most gossip magazines even without a single source to verbally confirm the news for them. It doesn't matter anymore, though. It's been a while now since Tristan's proposal, and I've learned firsthand that they were serious about the outcome. The diamond he slid on my finger is not a fake and still shines beautifully on my ring finger.

His brow smooths as he looks me over. I've noticed it happens whenever someone questions him, or he becomes irritated. Tristan doesn't show many of his emotions toward anyone else when he becomes pissed off, but I've been able to pick up a few tells when it comes to his brothers and me.

"It's proper, Kresley. You don't get engaged and not host a party to formally announce it."

"Oh the scandal," I mutter, my hand coming to my mouth in mock outrage and roll my eyes. He may have been raised to know these things and follow high society guidelines, but I wasn't. We're rich, but we've never been *that* wealthy to need to know these specific rules of etiquette.

He stops abruptly, his grip on my hand tightening as he spins me in, tucking me close to him. "It is when it comes to my family. You're one of us now, or you will be soon enough; you have to think of these things. No more living in the clouds, my beautiful fiancée. It may seem dumb to you, but this is important to my father and grandfather."

"No kidding." I sigh.

"What's that supposed to mean?" he questions, his free hand moving to pinch my chin and hold my face to his.

"It's different and overwhelming. I don't like being something I'm not." I have a habit of looking away and rolling my eyes when it comes to Tristan and his demands, but I need to open up to him more instead of just closing off. Things have gotten better between us. I've had time to get used to our engagement and his bulldozing nature, but I still haven't learned to completely bite my tongue around him. Turning away to roll my eyes avoids us arguing, but he's been starting to catch on and call me out. I have to broach subjects carefully and figure out how to prevent it from turning into an argument of push and pull.

"I understand, darling, but in time you'll adapt. It'll soon be second nature to you as it is for my brothers and me."

"I know you have security on me," I admit, bringing up a subject that's been riding on my shoulders.

His body stiffens, his gaze raking over my face. He's already gearing up for a fight.

I continue. "If one of you isn't with me running or shopping or whatever else I may be doing, then you have a security detail on me. I know they've attempted to be sneaky, but I've caught them several times. They're especially conspicuous in the mornings. You expect me to believe fit men have just randomly decided to run at the same time I do every morning? And not just some random guy; it's always three or four of them. What gives, Tristan? I've been fine on my own for years."

He releases a breath. Rather than reprimanding me, he leans his forehead against mine sweetly and closes his eyes. It's a very un-Tristan like move but not one I don't enjoy. He's the most stubborn boy I've ever met—besides Brent. "Word has spread about us outside of the academy and this little town. People all over the country amongst others have had plenty of time to find out exactly who you are, as well as your habits." His lids part, rewarding me with his slate irises and I bite my lip, not wanting to add to his worry.

"Okay...but it's never mattered before."

"You weren't mine, sugar plum. You are now. You're my fiancée. My father has many enemies...*MANY*. I won't let someone have the chance of hurting you to get to my father. It's not only you; we all have security teams if we're going out somewhere alone. They do their best to be discreet so we can attempt to live a somewhat semi-normal life, but they can't be completely invisible. That would be impossible." His gaze skirts off to the sides, and he says, "Look, we're going to be late. We can discuss this more later if needed. Let's get to class." He presses a chaste kiss to my lips, and I nod, letting it go for now. I'll definitely be bringing this up again. For the moment he's given me something, and that's far more than what he usually offers.

"A party?" Sam exclaims a little too excitedly when I share the engagement announcement news with her at the end of the day. Tristan didn't once mention that I couldn't share the news with anyone, so of course, I'm telling Sam all about it. I'm sure he's fully aware that I share practically everything with her anyhow; she's my best friend, after all.

"Mmm," I nod unenthusiastically, shoving my academy tablet, sweater, and pens back in my locker. I grab my purse and dig out my Porsche fob before closing and locking my other belongings away. Today's a rare occasion. I don't have homework from any of my classes so I can leave everything behind in my locker and not lug anything home with me. The time between Thanksgiving and Christmas break is mostly focused on in-class tests and tablet assignments. The end of the year is usually the same way as well.

"This is going to be awesome. I love extravagant parties. Is it cocktail or formal wear, and where's it located? Did he give you many details? Gah, this is exciting!"

"From what I managed to get out of Tristan during class, is that it's formal wear definitely and it'll be in their home ballroom."

"Holy shit, they're actually letting people come to their house?

I thought they were obsessed with their privacy?"

"Hey, that's not completely true. I go to their house, remember?" I stick out my tongue and follow it up with a smirk.

"Yeah, yeah, I know. *But* you're pretty much the only person they let in the door. I've overheard several of the guys and girls chatting about how they've tried to get an invite, but none of the guys ever extend one."

"Ugh, I'm so tired of the gossip. Besides, they're private people. You'd think everyone would want to embrace and respect that concept. Imagine *Twilight* but without the sparkling vampires," I find myself defending. They're super wealthy, the next level type and their dad doesn't have the most upstanding job. I can see why they're hesitant about allowing people into their personal space. I'd probably be the same way to an extent if it were my family in possible jeopardy.

"*Please*, the de Lacharrieres put Edward and Jacob to shame, so I'd have to imagine *Twilight* on a dose of souped-up steroids."

She's completely right, the guys have way more money and far better looks, but I have no idea what else I could use as an example to compare to their privacy level.

"Well, if it makes you feel special, Sam, it's not being held at the house across from mine that I'm always at. I found out Mr. de Lacharriere only bought that place for them to stay in temporarily while their massive new mansion was being built. Apparently, it took longer than usual houses because of the vast size and opulence."

Cole took me to the new place already so he could switch out from the Ashton Martin he frequently drives around. He has two that he loves the most, the matte black Vanquish and also the extravagant pearl white One 77. His other vehicles are parked at the mansion because the garage is enormous. They could probably comfortably fit twenty cars or more inside. I was shocked, to say the least. I don't know how to articulate the feeling I got being surrounded by someone's personal car lot. The mini castle is finished now, of course, but it's being deep cleaned, professionally decorated and then stocked with anything and everything they could require before the family moves their clothes and any other various belongings in.

"The ballroom is absolutely stunning and humongous. I've seen that since it was one of the first rooms to be designed. I guess if we're going to have a huge, pretentious party that would be the best place to organize and hold it at, aside from a rented venue."

"Yeah, but the party is supposed to be for you and Tristan as a couple. Shouldn't you both be the ones to decide where it's held and when?"

Shrugging, I offer up a bland smile and rationalize, "His father's paying for it."

And truthfully, I really don't care about the time, place, or date Tristan's father and his party planners decide to use. I'm not going to waste my time fretting over those trivial details, but rather, do what I need to for myself and my well-being. I'm going to attempt to gain my focus back on maintaining the good grades I have and raise them higher so I'll be offered a full scholarship to college. These boys have basically consumed my attention when I should've been using it on school. I don't know what our marriage will look like in the future, and I don't want to be completely dependent on Tristan or his father's money for anything I may need or desire.

Sam releases a sigh, linking her arm through mine as we head out back toward the field. My best friend's so nosey, and I know she wants to have her hands in everything. Especially since the party and wedding is for me, her closest friend. It doesn't matter who ends up paying for the ceremony. She'll figure out a way to be involved, aside from being my maid of honor. That's one thing I can't wait for, to ask her to stand up next to me at the altar when I have to exchange my vows with Tristan. I'll be so nerve-racked with the importance and implications of that day; having her near me throughout the day will help immensely.

"Football's nearly over. That means you'll have more free time to spend with your guys. I hope they realize that we're a package deal. Whether they have you holed up at their new house or not, I need some time with my best friend. Shopping, movies, nails...you know how we roll on break. I don't care if they tag along, but no keeping you to themselves."

"I won't let them suck up all my time, no matter how bossy they are. I promise. We'll still do our usual stuff, and you're completely right, they may tag along for some things. I could see us talking Axel into a pedicure, Brent and Cole into movies, and Tristan with the shopping. You may be tired of them by the end of break," I tease. "Oh, and speaking of shopping, the party will be before winter break. It'll kind of be like a formal engagement announcement, but also a holiday celebration thrown into the mix."

She squeals, yanking my arm into her to squeeze with her excitement. "This is going to be so much fun and formal...we'll have to use your fiancé's black card when we go shopping. With your complexion and the timing, we can put you in a deep red gown. You will look freaking amazing! Any of these bitches that've been giving you trouble who attend with their parents will be foaming at the mouth with jealousy. In fact, they're lucky I don't put you in white or gold just to be extra ostentatious! We have to find something to show off your long neck and sexy collarbone. The boys will just die!"

I can't help but giggle at her enthusiasm. "Still, ball gowns at Christmas...ugh, don't you think it's just a tad on the extra pretentious side?"

My mother will be absolutely thrilled at the chance to show off in front of the other wealthy attendees. This isn't an engagement celebration to them, but a chance to rub elbows with people outside their usual social circles and bank tier. My father will treat it as a business deal in the works, of course, while I'll be doing my best to hide away and remain out of the spotlight. The last thing I want is to be in the papers and online even more so than Tristan's well-planned engagement stunt months back at the club. The moment word gets out about an uber wealthy family coughing up a son for a marriage agreement to a lesser prominent family, it'll be piranhas chomping at the bit to dig out any possible dirty secret on us. They'll want to destroy my family by running a smear campaign, and the students at Harvard Academy will eat it up. I've seen how this works in the past with other people, and I want none of it.

A snort and an eye roll later, Sam's grabbing my arm and toting me toward Axel's waiting form, all while naming the reasons why the rich do what they do. The one thing she points out that has me on edge is that I better get used to it all. It may be Tristan and his family's money, but soon enough, I'll be sharing his last name, and by extension, people will believe I'm filthy rich as well.

Chapter Eleven

"Welcome and thank you for joining us at our new home," the quad's father boasts, as my parents, my younger brother, and I follow him into the recently decorated dining room. We each take our designated seat and sit down to have dinner. The dining room is enormous enough that we could probably host our engagement party in this room, let alone the expansive ballroom.

"Great place you have here." Father compliments to be polite, though I can read the envy that's consuming his gaze. No doubt in my mind that he's thinking of himself living here and not the de Lacharrieres. "Though I suppose Kresley won't be staying here but will move wherever Tristan decides to attend college."

I bite down on my tongue hard enough to draw blood at Father's flippant comment. Of course, he'd automatically think I'd give up my goals and any choices about my future to follow Tristan wherever he may want to go. He expects me to be a dutiful wife and do as my husband pleases. This is precisely one of the reasons why I've wanted to escape his grasp as soon as possible. He so quickly makes decisions over my entire existence as if it belongs to him alone, and I don't have a voice. *I have to get that scholarship so I can decide on my own fate.* Of course, I'll marry Tristan; Father would strangle me if I didn't. However, my future husband has to get used to the idea that I won't sit back idly. I deserve to have a chance at an education and career as well, just like everyone else in America has when they work hard.

Tristan beams approvingly at my dad, and his father simply agrees with mine. It's all far too simple how they act, not one of them pausing to even consider what I may desire. Axel flashes me a sympathetic look, but Cole and Brent simply stare at their father, waiting for the master to speak to them, I suppose. I can't help but silently question myself repeatedly, *is this really my life?* It is for another year and a half at least. Then they can try to stop me and stand in my way. I don't care if I have to wait tables, shelve books, scrub toilets, or whatever, to survive while in college. I'll do what I have to to make it happen for myself.

"We have the engagement announcement party next week. I thought now would be a perfect time to consider wedding dates." The oldest de Lacharriere continues with a flippant wave, and my neck grows warm with tension. I'm only a junior in high school, and they're ready to put the nail in my coffin when it comes to giving me away to another. Some people don't marry until they're in their thirties or older, and here I'm being shoved head first into matrimony at age seventeen.

Mother smiles pleasantly and speaks up, though this deal is clearly between the two men seated at opposite ends of the table. She likes to pretend that they give two thoughts to what she thinks. "I'd like to wait until after Kresley is eighteen."

My mouth gapes, dumbfounded by her sensible suggestion and uncharacteristic behavior.

The boys' father scoffs, his gaze sharpening in on the frail woman. He looks like he could eat Mom for lunch and not skip a beat. "Nonsense, a year's engagement is customary in these arrangements. No reason for it to go any longer and put off the inevitable. Unless, of course, it's finances you're concerned about."

Dad opens his mouth to argue or else reassure him that we have the funds, and Mom butts in again. "I agree, but in this case, it'll be more of scandal than anything else. If we have a wedding during the school year, everyone will be holding their breath to see if Kresley is secretly pregnant. I won't have my daughter's name tarnished, and I'm sure you wouldn't want the same for your son either. Reputations mean everything in certain circumstances."

"You have a point..." He trails off, finger tapping his chin in contemplation and Mom beams in her small triumph.

"After graduation, the weather will be perfect for a late spring/early summer wedding ceremony. Maybe in the Hamptons then. They won't have to worry about when they'll go on a honeymoon or move away for college."

My father raps the table and says, "Think of the excitement you'll drum up while everyone attempts to get on the invite list."

Great. My wedding's going to turn into a damn circus production with tickets being sold to the highest bidder, rather than full of people who actually give a shit about Tristan and me. This has become one big mess since this proposal production began at the club. Now it's even worse because I'm starting to have real feelings involved where the boys are concerned. Tristan has made it loud and clear that he plans to marry me no matter what I have to say about it. Brent, Cole, and Axel go right along with him. They act as if it's the most normal thing in the world, but I can't help to wonder how the guys feel inside about the entire thing. Do they truly care? Do they like me as much as I find myself liking them?

Rather than voice my opinions on the subject, I sit quietly, keeping to myself. I won't risk Father's wrath by suggesting we wait to get married. At least postpone to after we all graduate college or something, but that'll never happen. It's hard to believe that in this room, I'm the rational thinking person. A nudge to my shin has me jerking, meeting the gaze of the boy in front of me. Tristan winks, and I roll my eyes in return. This subject seems entirely far too entertaining to everyone, especially my betrothed.

"It's settled then," Mr. de Lacharriere booms. "The engagement announcement celebration will be a holiday-themed event, and we'll plan for the wedding ceremony to be shortly after they graduate."

My stomach churns with nerves. I slide my chair back and stand to my feet, garnering everyone's attention. I clear my throat, nearly stuttering to Tristan's intimidating father. "Please excuse me. I need to use the ladies room."

He smiles wide, his features sharp and calculating. He really does remind me of a shark, and it has me swallowing with nerves, my throat feeling tight and dry under his scrutiny. With a quick jerk of his chin, he orders, "Son, escort your fiancée to the restroom."

The last thing I wanted was any of the males at this table to encroach on my nerve-wracked peeing time, but it's better than having to sit here in the midst of the adults selling my soul. Tristan comes to my side, politely offering his elbow. Gratefully, he's not being an asshat in the moment; I offer a shaky smile in return.

"Come on, beautiful," he encourages. I slide my hand into the crook of his elbow, admiring his muscular arm in the process. He's a big guy; he'll be an even bigger man when it's all said and done. There's something about that weird fact that's sexy to me.

He grins, pleased that I've taken him up on his peace offering. I know better than to turn him down. Tristan could make my life difficult quite easily if he wished. I've had a rough enough time at school lately to want to add any more fuel to the fire. He murmurs once we've left the dining room and nosey ears of our families behind. "Are you okay? Your cheeks were pinker than usual."

His attention and knowledge on my 'tells' has me blushing more than I already was. With a shrug, I quietly admit, "It's overwhelming to listen to them plan our future like that. Doesn't it bother you at all?"

He copies me, shrugging his massive shoulders. I feel small, feminine, and protected at his side. It's a scary thought, knowing

I've grown so comfortable around him already. "It's been like this my whole life, so I guess I'm used to it."

"I wish I could be so blasé about it all."

He turns to me, his palm moving to softly cup my cheek as he says, "You could be, you know? If you would finally just let your guard down and trust me, you would see that I want this—that I want you."

I gaze up into his misty gray eyes. It's so easy to get lost in them. He's far too handsome for his own good. He's got so much confidence and swagger emanating from him that it makes him stand out from his brothers. This man is someone who could have the world on his shoulders, and you'd never know it. He'd stroll through it with ease, wearing a charming, natural smile. "Part of me actually believes you, you know," I confess and suddenly he seems so much closer. He's breathing my air and taking up my space, his body heat warming me all over.

"And the other part?" he whispers, his nose almost touching mine.

"Tells me that not everything is what it seems to be."

"You're right; it's not." Tristan stuns me by saying, "It's so much more. More than you'll ever guess, my darling." Then his demanding mouth is on mine, his tongue and taste, causing me to forget his admission.

I'm nothing when it comes to these guys having their hands or lips on me. I turn to mush, my hormones blazing like an inferno inside my core. I want him. I want them all. And I won't hesitate to take anything Tristan or his brothers are willing to give.

His hand slides to the back of my neck, his large palm easily anchoring me in place so he can consume as he wishes. I'm his for the taking, and he doesn't hesitate even for a moment to let me know exactly what he's thinking. His free hand wraps behind me, embracing my frame to his mass and his fingers move to firmly cup my ass and lift me to where he wants me. He brings me even closer to his body, if that's possible, as he shifts, seeking out the apex of my thighs.

Tristan's hips tilt forward and back, his grinding force allowing my lower tummy and core to rub against the bulky bulge in his trousers. He molds our forms together. Any closer and we'd fuse as one, but it still doesn't seem like enough, as desire skyrockets through me. His cock is firm, and with the added pressure from his hips and tight grip on my ass, I can tell he's long and thick. It'll hurt me when he finally takes me as his wife...or before.

In this game, I'm Tristan's to do with as he wishes. No matter how hard I may try to resist or don't, it's the reality of my situation. I'm lucky he hasn't decided to push me for more, to take it further than he has in this moment right now. Or am I? I can't help but crave his caresses on my flesh, to desire his annoying bossiness and steamrolling nature. I want to feel him everywhere, to have all of him. If only I weren't so utterly consumed by his touch, maybe...just maybe, I'd have taken his words as a warning.

Chapter Twelve

"It's the first day of winter break; tell me you're doing something to make your heart race, beba." Cole rasps into the phone. His deep baritone gives me all the feelings when I'm relaxed and talking to him like this.

"Nope and I'm not even a little bit sorry about it either," I share with a laugh. "Sam has already dragged me out into town. We stopped in for a last-minute fitting for my party dress, and my mom will have people in tomorrow to do our nails, hair, and makeup. She wants them to be fresh for the party."

Once I told Sam about the announcement celebration, she'd scavenged the internet and her various favorite designers to find me a dress. She'd acquired the perfect gown for me almost immediately. It was a little scary how fast she was able to do it as her shopping has reached an entirely new level of expertise. I wasn't complaining, though. It was one less thing I had to worry about. All I had to do was take it in to be fitted and adjusted as needed. My mom even went as far as seeking Sam's advice on what color she should wear herself. I was completely shocked and happy for my friend, as my mom's snobbish and stuck-up where her clothes are concerned.

"*Boring* mon belle," he groans, and my smile widens. I've learned to appreciate Cole's laid-back ways. Where everyone else seems to be putting on a show for someone around, Cole just doesn't give a shit about anything except himself. I wish I could do the same; it has to feel so freeing to just wake up and say, *I'm wearing sweats to school today. To hell with the uniform or what anyone else thinks.* My family, along with Cole's, wouldn't know what to do if they were to be put in a situation like that. Everyone's always so uptight and on edge about something.

"Fine. Maybe it's boring to you, Mr. Race Car Driver, but I'm determined to stay in these warm, fuzzy pajamas all day long."

"Mm, yeah, beba."

"What's that supposed to mean?"

"Just picturing you in pajamas, mon belle."

"Oh?"

"Yep, and not the warm, fuzzy kind."

My cheeks heat. "Well, these are, so you're far off."

He chuckles and the delicious, gravely rasp gives me goosebumps. "I bet you're adorable, beba."

Wearing a goofy smile, I glance down at the full body fluffy sheep pajamas and burst into giggles. "You have no idea." Since the whole car debacle, I've grown much more comfortable with Cole. I find myself closer and closer to each guy as the days pass. They're quickly becoming my favorite people. The girls at school are envious but have backed off a significant amount since I befriended the cheer squad. The guys who treated me like I had a contagious disease are polite but keep their respectable distance. I've heard from Sam that any guy who expresses interest in me, Brent hunts them down. I've never witnessed it personally, and have argued about it, but she swears it's true.

"How 'bout you come on outside?"

"I knew you were driving."

"You think you know me now, huh?"

"Maybe..." I flirt.

"Come get in the car, beba."

"Why? Where are we going?"

"I'm taking your sexy pajama ass to get a milk shake."

"It's winter," I argue to the crazy dude wanting ice cream when the temperatures are freezing outside.

"Yep, it's the best time to have them. You can ask my podnas on that one. Now move it. I want to see your sexy ass and feed you a milk shake. You can keep your pajamas on; we'll hit up drive-thru and chill."

"So romantic," I joke, pulling my hood up and skipping down the stairs, not letting on that I'm giving in to his peer pressure.

"I could lick the ice cream off you..."

"Cole!" I gasp as my mother's inquisitive gaze meets mine.

Her eyebrow rises, intrigued, and I quickly fill in, "Cole's taking me for ice cream."

She shakes her head, disapprovingly. "You have a party tomorrow, Kresley, one that you need to look your absolute best at. Plus, you can't leave our house looking like that." She flicks her gaze over my sheepish self, wearing a sneer. "I can't believe someone from camp bought you those horrendous things as a thank-you gift." She shakes her head at the ridiculous outfit, and my grin instantly falls flat.

Of course, she wouldn't understand it. No one around here knows the real me, the one who doesn't care about reaching the top one percent hierarchy in the country. Cole honks the horn and says into the phone, "Tell her I told you to wear them."

"Uh, Cole asked me to wear them. It's a-a silly thing we're doing."

Mother scoffs with disbelief. "Really, Cole de Lacharriere's doing this?"

I nod and swallow. I'm under enough pressure with tomorrow coming much quicker than I'd like, and yet she can't let me have a little fun and attempt to relax. I wish everyone wasn't so determined to come off as perfect. "We're driving. I mean, we're staying in the car. Just getting a shake and then he wanted to drive me out to show me this cool ice thing he discovered. No one will see me looking like this."

She waves her hand in a shoo motion. "Fine. Just don't be too late. You need rest, and don't you dare get sick. There's only so much makeup can cover, you know."

"I won't, I promise."

"Go. Have some fun." She tilts her head, and I jog past wearing a smile once again. I'm nearly out the door when she calls, "Tell Cole hello and make sure you thank him for paying attention to you."

"Bye!" I yell.

Cole mutters at the same time. "Don't tell me shit. Of course, I'm paying attention to you. Anyone not is fucking stupid. You're beautiful," he growls, then I'm skidding around the big, black SUV and climbing into the front seat.

"Oh my God, it's freezing out there!" I admonish then turn toward the now silent Cole. "What?" I ask, rubbing my cold hands together and over my chilled cheeks. I was only outside for a moment, and I'm shivering, How can he want ice cream in this?

He licks his lips, his mouth tilting into an amused grin. "Beba," he admonishes with a chuckle.

My face is on fire with his teasing. It only takes one word from him and a look, and I can read everything he's holding back. If it were his brothers, I'm not sure they'd hold back the teasing so much. "I told you they were terrible."

"Nah, you're too cute like this."

"You think so?" I ask, tucking my hair behind my ear.

Cole leans his long body across my front to grab the seat belt. He buckles me in, our faces so close to one another that our breath mingles. His tastes like orange soda and it makes me wish he'd kiss me. "Safety first, and yeah," he says and leans back, putting the giant vehicle in gear.

My heart beat increases at his admission and at our closeness. Every bit of my body was screaming for him to touch me, to kiss me, but I know he couldn't. My family could've seen us, and that wouldn't have ended well at all.

"I was thinking you'd be in pajamas, too, since you told me to keep mine on."

He turns onto the street using one hand while reaching across to place his palm on my leg. We've been in the car together several times now, so his touch is comfortable. "Nope, just didn't want to wait while you changed."

I snort.

"Plus, I wanted to catch you not so *put together*."

"Please, you've seen me running. I'm a hot, sweaty mess. It seems like you always find me when I'm not expecting it."

Cole shrugs. "I think you're lovely like that." He says it with such finality like there is no other option in his mind.

His compliment has me smitten with my smile growing thoughtful as I point out, "You're in a sweet mood today."

"Yeah?" He squeezes my leg, and I nod, licking my lips. How can I get like this around each one of them? It's not normal to be equally enthralled by four different guys all at once.

Cole pulls into the drive-thru, orders, pays and then hands over a shake.

"How do you know what flavor I like?" I take the offered straw and push it in the lid, slurping a drink of the thick, sugary concoction.

He shrugs. "I don't."

"Oh..."

"I ordered you my favorite," he says, and my eyes shoot to him.

He doesn't turn to me, but I'm content with just watching him drive. He has something playing on the radio that's low enough I can hear a soft thump-thump come through the speakers. It's relaxing being like this with him, wrapped in his scent and my comfy sheep pajamas. I'd never have expected this tonight, and it's a pleasant surprise.

We drive for a while before he eventually pulls off the road. I take my eyes away from his handsome profile to glance around. The overlook is breathtaking with different sized trees all full of powdery white snow. The many hills surrounding the secluded area appear to be untouched, even by the wildlife. I'm sure most of the animals are sleeping anyhow, snuggled up in their body heat and burrows. It's almost loud out here with how quiet it is, being alone with Cole, surrounded by so much freshly fallen snow.

"Wow," I finally manage to breathe out after taking it all in and processing the true beauty of nature.

Cole nods and admits, "I thought of you when I first saw it. All dressed up to look perfect and untouched. When the snow melts, though, it's an entirely different sight."

"You think I'm like that?"

His crystal blue irises fall to me, "You stand out from anyone around you. Kresley, you're so put together and perfect all the time...but no one knows you're even more striking underneath it all. They only see the shiny layer, not the rest, mon cher."

He clicks his tongue, slowly running his gaze over every inch of me it seems. It's so intimate; it feels more like a caress. Leaning in, he draws my lower lip between his, sucking. "Mm," he groans. "So fucking delicious."

"It's the milk shake," I mumble with a smile, and he grins, his mouth still against mine.

"I know, beba. Why'd you think I wanted it so badly? Been thinking about tasting it on your tongue."

His words have me flushing and exhaling with a desire filled sigh. There's a snap noise, and my seat belt retracts.

"What..." I begin to ask, but Cole cuts me off as his hands move to my hips.

His grip tightens as he lifts me over the center console and our drinks, planting me firmly on his lap. His face dips in, nuzzling into my neck. His breath on my flesh provokes goosebumps to overtake my body again. My breasts swell, and my nipples tighten to stiff peaks; he has to be able to feel them through my pajamas and his shirt as I'm not wearing a bra.

"I want to feel you, beba," he whispers, and his hand moves to unzip the front of my pajamas.

Sitting back, I put some distance between us, and my hands stall his movements. "Cole..."

"All good, mon cher, I promise."

"Wait, what are you doing?"

"I'm having my milk shake," he practically purrs, continuing to slide the zipper down. Pushing the material aside, he exposes my breasts. "Fuck," he curses with longing. Peppering kisses on the flesh above my breasts, he punctuates, "So. Damn. Sweet."

Oh God, I can't believe I'm letting him do this. Though, I suppose you don't let the de Lacharrieres do anything. They have no rules or limits it appears—at least, this one doesn't.

"Lean against the wheel, beba."

I do as he instructs, his hands drawing my thighs to rest on each side of him. Moisture pools between my thighs, and I can't help but wonder if I'll embarrassingly leave any behind on his light-colored sweats. The position is incredibly intimate, and my body's aware of every inch that's touching his. His lips leave my flesh as he grabs the large foam cup of milk shake. He ordered the biggest they had, and I swear I've never seen a cup so large. Opening the lid, he grabs a plastic spoon and gets just a small amount on the spoon before moving it toward me.

Holding my breath in anticipation, my body trembles with pent-up sexual desire as he touches the bit of shake to the peak of my nipple. A gasp escapes at the sudden coldness, and then his warm, wet mouth is on me. The heat of his tongue surrounds my nipple as he sucks and nibbles the creamy concoction off my skin. No one has ever done anything remotely close to my body before, and it has my core throbbing with the intense sensations.

"Oh!" I breathe as he shifts to do the same thing to the opposite nipple, following up with small soft laps. "Shit, that's so good."

"Mm," Cole groans, sucking like he can't get enough.

His hips tilt upward, encouraging my body to grind against his as he has his fill. His tongue plays with my nipple until I'm nearly writhing in his lap. The sensations are enthralling, making me lose my inhibitions. I'm silently praying he removes all of my clothes to lick the milk shake from every part of me. At this point, I won't protest if he does. I want his mouth to taste all of me.

Repeatedly, he pulls away to refill his spoon, place the milk shake on my nipple, and then clean the sugary coldness off me with his mouth. Each time that he moves away, I whimper, wanton with need for more. By the seventh time, I'm moaning loudly. My hips angle and grind my clit against his hardness, no longer attempting to refrain from the pleasure. He's so attentive and sexy that he makes my core all wet and needy, craving more of his touch.

"Cole!" I call breathily, and his arm wraps around my waist. He holds me tightly, his lithe muscles moving me where he wants. "Oh!" I whimper as he shifts upward, his thickness hitting me in the perfect spot. He pushes my hips to grind upward while drawing me downward, sliding against me. His hardness presses my button and juices flood my core as my orgasm hits me out of nowhere. "Yes!" I yell. My forehead falls to his shoulder as I ride the wave of bliss, sliding against his length. I wish he was inside me, stretching and filling me.

Cole grunts, tucking his face into my neck. It turns me on more, hearing him like this and feeling his breath on the skin under my ear. My body trembles as I quake with my last little hit of orgasm high. He shudders with me in his arms, and I can't help but wonder if he lost control as well. One thing is for sure, I'll never be able to look at a milk shakes in the same way ever again without thinking of Cole and what happened tonight.

He leans back, and his hold eases. Cole's sparkling cobalt irises meet mine. "Damn, mon cher, I can't seem to hold back with you. My brothers would give me shit if they knew I lost it in my pants." He grins, and I laugh as it eventually registers.

Tilting forward, I brush my eager lips against his full mouth. It's far too comfortable being with him like this and it shouldn't be. But I'm no longer fooling myself; I know it's easy being intimate with each of the guys, almost as if it was meant to be. However, I can't believe I just orgasmed on Cole's lap when I'm going to be celebrating my engagement to his brother tomorrow. I let it go too far this time. Sure they kiss me, but this seems like we're moving toward a lot more and I'm not sure how Tristan or myself will feel about that step. "Wow, that was-that was really good," I admit with a whisper and he pecks a soft kiss on my lips again, agreeing.

"Yeah, sure was, beba. I'm gonna hop out really quick and see if I have a spare pair of pants in the back." He taps my thigh, and I nod, scooting back over the center console and into my seat.

Cole's door closes, and I'm left alone with my thoughts. I'm completely lost, falling head first for the guys individually. I'm supposed to be marrying their brother but stuck in wanting them all. I'm so confused, and I'm being pulled in every direction. Zipping up my pajamas, I can't help but close my eyes and reminisce of how his mouth felt on me moments ago. That was beyond amazing, and I find myself craving more, even if I know I shouldn't.

"Fuck, it's cold out there!" he comments, grumbling as he slides back into the driver's side and blasts the heater. "One thing I miss about Louisiana for sure is warm winters."

"Was it hard leaving there to come all the way up here?" I haven't brought up their old home. I wasn't sure if it'd be a sore subject since they don't mention it much, if ever. They tend to keep to themselves about all things that involve personal stuff—even to me—and I'm around them more than anyone else from school.

His irises sparkle as he looks me over, taking in every detail. He zeros in on my chest and the fact that I've zipped myself back into my fuzzy, warm pajamas. "You know better than anyone mon cher, that my father enjoys mapping out futures."

"Yours included?"

Cole swallows and then nods. He remains tight-lipped about the subject, and I take the hint that he doesn't want to delve any deeper into it. I respect his feelings and leave it at that. I know better than anyone of how it feels to not want to share details of your home life or your parents.

Slurping, I take in a big gulp of the thick, cool mixture of my chocolate peanut butter explosion milk shake and let it coat my throat. I use the sugar for a little courage and broach, "Cole...about what just happened," I begin, and his brows rise in anticipation.

"What about it, beba?"

"Well, tomorrow is the party, and I'm not sure if I should be doing this sort of thing with Tristan and me being publicly engaged now."

"Tell me something...do you like us?"

"Of course," I admit immediately. "I wasn't sure at first. Especially because you were brash with your outspokenness and Brent was irritable or wrapped up in a similar mood. That's changed though; you've each opened up to me more and showed me there's more to you guys."

Cole repeats the question, but rewords it a bit and with emphasis. "Do you *like-like* us? And all of us, or just a few?"

I grab my shake, gulping down a few mouthfuls of frozen, creamy sugar. Staring intently at my foam cup, I contemplate on what to say. Should I tell him the truth along with finally admitting it aloud to myself? I've fought my feelings from the second they became complicated, thinking it was wrong to want them the way I do. I don't know how much longer I can fight it, though, and after a moment, I whisper, "Yes."

"Relax mon cher, we all *like* you too. We've told you before, Kresley; you belong to all of us."

"B-but how does that work if I'm marrying Tristan?" I ask, feeling even more confused now that it's out in the open with Cole. "I don't want to hurt him or make him upset before we're even married. I mean...you're his brothers. It has to be weird for him and each of you as well."

"Has anyone told you it was strange or did Tristan tell you he was disappointed about it?"

I shake my head. None of them have even hinted that it's abnormal or that they're troubled about our shared affections. The only times I've heard them say anything about it is back when Brent walked into Axel's room and reminded him that I'm set to marry Tristan. Me overhearing it was awkward enough, and thankfully the subject was never brought up around me again.

"Look, we told you before that you're ours. I'm not sure if you've noticed or not, but we like to share and often. Not everything, but some things we'd rather have even a little piece of, versus none at all. You get what I'm saying? It's difficult to explain?"

"I think so..."

"Unless one of us straight out tells you we don't like you or that we're jealous, please trust us. Oddly enough, we know what we're doing when it comes to you and how we want it to be. Each of us want you, beba, so this way we all get to have you."

With a nervous breath, I ask, "And tomorrow?"

"Nothing changes. You wear Tristan's ring, and for appearance purposes, you stick close to him. In private, you will still belong to all of us."

I have to know. Is this only until we say our vows? Is there a time limit? "For how long, Cole? Does this have an expiration date?"

"Why are you worrying so much? Like I mentioned before, you need to have faith in us. We will always take care of you."

Swallowing, I sigh and look away. I try to trust them, and with time, it's becoming easier. Now they're asking me to confide in them with my heart, and that's a different story entirely. I'm afraid I'll fall completely for all four of them, and then three of them will turn their backs on me. I've needed them on my side for this marriage, against my father and their own. I've also needed them to be a buffer with Tristan. Now, I need them, so my heart won't break.

That realization is scarier than any marriage or rich man planning my future.

Chapter Thirteen

"Today's the big day, Kresley. Aren't you positively thrilled for the opulent party?" Mom asks as the first set of stylists begins on our hair.

Two nail techs gather their supplies along with portable pedicure tubs to begin on our pedi's. Winter months or not, mother swears that women are supposed to always have soft feet and pretty toes no matter the season. She says feet are ugly enough to not stay on top of taking care of their appearance. Personally, they don't bother me. She'd be appalled if she discovered I'd previously had an in-depth conversation on feet and toes with Axel. We were swimming and got on the subject, and he knows pretty much everything there is about everything, so we get distracted easily on random topics.

Rubbing my eyes sleepily, I mumble, "Not thrilled enough to be woken up at eight a.m. I'm pretty sure all of this could've waited an extra two or three hours."

I rarely voice any objections. I learned long ago they practically mean nothing to my parents. I'm a grouchy morning person, though, and can't hold back when she asks.

"Nonsense!" She waves me off as if my mind's too small to understand anything when it comes to being a woman. "Of course it had to be first thing. It's been far too long since you had your roots updated, and while I'm not fond of the lavender shade, it's a trend right now, and you need to keep up appearances. You really should pay more attention, Kresley."

The one blessing of having snobby parents is I get to have light lavender hair to be on the "cusp of trends." They may think I'm keeping up appearances for their sake, but in reality, it was one minor way I could be different from all the other rich kids. I don't want to blend in with the stepford academy students. I'm much more than them inside. Not in a stuck-up way, but in a "I don't belong with you type of people" sort of way. I want so much more in my life than what they have in store.

"You're bleaching my roots?" I complain, knowing the time and itchiness I have in store with the chore.

My stylist chuckles before saying, "You'll be in like a bazillion photos *honey,* you have to be *fly AF,* and you know my work needs to be looking top-notch on that *fabulous* head of yours." He's super gay, like wear a rainbow shirt every day and eyeliner kind. I love him; he always has a good attitude and makes me feel pretty, even when he's yanking on my hair.

"Ouch!" I cry as the tiny lady kneeling at my feet stabs into my big toe with her sharp tool.

She shoots me a look before grumbling, "You have ingrown nail. How you girl is beyond me."

I send her a sheepish smile before shrugging. "I run a lot."

"No kidding. Your feet like hippo."

Mom glares at me as if I can help having runner's feet. It's the one joy I get, and this cute oriental lady is throwing me under the bus. The next nail she yanks out I better keep my mouth closed, or Mom'll be tossing my runners into the trash. I'd have to resort to bribing Sam to order me a new pair if that happened.

"I'm starving. Please tell me we aren't fasting all day." I hate it when she makes us not eat before the party. I show up light-headed and feeling rabid at the site of food. Not to mention my stomach makes all these crazy gurgling noises, and if there's no music playing, it's incredibly embarrassing.

"Of course, we aren't eating. You had a milk shake yesterday, so you'll be bloated enough in your gown."

Sighing, I blow off her response. She'll be even more nitpicky than usual today. I'm in for a full spread of yanking, dyeing, washing, plucking, painting, and prepping. I am a bit excited about tonight, though. I'm not looking forward to the announcement portion or the random jerks that are invited. Nor my mother's constant watch, expecting me to be perfect, but I should be able to escape her at some point, hopefully. On the upside, I get to see my quads dressed to the nines and that's had me conjuring up delicious images of them since it was announced that it's a formal affair.

My best friend blows into Mom's dressing room like a tornado full of sunshine and dark hair. The room's attached to her massive closet and en suite. "Morning!" she beams cheerily, and I want to toss a brush or something at her. She's carrying beverages, though, so hopefully, it's something good. "I know there won't be any eating involved today so I brought smoothies." She must've got my text when I woke up, thank fuck! My best friend is seriously the best.

"Oh, thank God!" I exclaim, making a hasty grab for the entire tray.

She giggles as Mom begins to chastise me and tell me I can't have any of it.

Sam argues. "Kresley can drink it, I promise. It's actually a cleansing smoothie that helps break down fat throughout the day. Her stomach will be nice and flat in time for the party."

Mom's eyes grow wide. "That sounds marvelous! Thank you for keeping her on track. Samantha!"

Sam smiles wickedly. "Of course!" She pushes the straw in and hands a large cup to me.

I take a long pull, and the flavors explode on my tongue. Sam's full of shit. This is a sunrise smoothie. There's no fat burning mumbo jumbo in it: just orange juice, strawberry, banana, fat free milk, vanilla yogurt, and ice. It's delicious to my starving tummy, and my mother has no idea. It's like breakfast in a glass, and it'll get me through a chunk of the day. Sam's a lifesaver; besides, I run a lot and need the healthy calories.

Mom thinks I'm reckless, but I've learned so much at camp each summer about what to and what not to put in my body. I know her random fasting isn't good for us. It just puts our body into survival mode, and it holds fat. I tried to tell her, but she wasn't having it. Rich people hate being wrong, so they pretend to know everything.

"How are you today?" Sam probes as she pulls up a chair beside me. My mom titters to her stylist in the background about her hair being the perfect shade.

"It's early," I gripe and she smirks with amusement.

"I don't think you'll ever change," she snickers and I agree. "I'm excited for tonight."

"Oh yeah? Did you ever find a date to bring?"

She releases a breath, biting her lip before admitting, "I did. *BUT* I didn't want to tell you before the party."

My forehead scrunches, and Mom butts in. "Stop that, or you'll get wrinkles!"

Instantly, my expression flattens, so my skin smooths back out, as I quietly ask, "What? Why not?" Taking a long pull of my smoothie, I try to hold still for my stylist and also lean in to listen.

She shrugs. "I just...I didn't want you to be uncomfortable or something. I figured if you didn't know until the party then you wouldn't worry about it. Plus you'll be extremely busy tonight, so I wanted to have someone there."

"Okay? I mean, of course, you should have a date, but why would I care who it is? I wanted you to bring someone, remember?"

She sits back, her freshly scrubbed face not needing an ounce of makeup no matter how early it is to look gorgeous. "Because it's Brandon."

"Wow." I'm surprised. I mean, sure he and I have spoken and cleared the air, but I wasn't expecting him to be there tonight. "I didn't think he'd want to come or I would've made sure he had an invitation. I should've sent one regardless."

"And he knows that; we already talked about it. He may not be happy about you being engaged," she coughs at the glower my mother shoots in our direction. "So, uh, soon, but he's still our friend. He wants to be there for you."

"I don't know what to say. I mean, if the roles were reversed, I'd want to be there to support him too. So, I get it. I'm just shocked he's come around this soon."

She nods. "We've actually been talking a lot more."

"Oh, really?"

She blushes, and my gaze takes her in again. She's all flustered from bringing him up. What's really going on between my friends? Just how much more could they be talking to make her act like this?

"Yeah, well, it's just that you're busier now." Her hand shoots up, her eyes growing wide. "Not in a bad way!" Sam amends before continuing, "I didn't mean it like that. I meant that you have the guys and they take up a lot of time."

I flick my eyes to my mom, and Sam quickly adds, "You have Tristan, which is awesome. He adores you, and I'm so happy for you. Anyhow, I've had some free time, and Brandon has too, so we've um, gotten closer."

My mouth tilts into a knowing grin, and I tease, "Uh huh, you *like* him."

Her lips pucker, her cheeks turning pink as if she's eating something sour and I can't help but laugh. My outspoken, charismatic best friend doesn't know what to do or say and it's hilarious. Maybe Brandon's exactly what she needs.

"How did I not see this before? He's practically the male version of you. No wonder I've always seen him as a brother!" My smile widens. "Oh my gawd, you two are perfect for each other!"

Her lips twist into a soft smile, and she glances away. Sam has it so bad. I hope he feels the same way about her. This is pretty perfect; I get my two best friends, and if they like each other, then the guys won't overreact with Brandon being near me anymore. They've grown pretty territorial over me being around other boys, especially Brandon. "I'm glad you're bringing him. The only thing I beg of you guys is not to break each other's hearts."

She rolls her eyes. "Please, that boy has nothing to worry about when it comes to me."

"Yeah?" I giggle. "This is so great."

"All right, enough about me already. This day is about you and that handsome hunk who gave you that gigantic rock on your finger."

My stylist leans in. "And that rock is total bling, *honey*! You tell that de Lacharriere the next diamond needs to be a canary or teal stone. It's all the rave right now."

Mom speaks up. "Stefan is right, Kresley, perhaps Tristan will gift you another for the wedding."

My smile drops. "One ring is plenty, thanks. I don't want to sink when I go swimming in the summer."

Mom's gasp sounds scandalized. "Don't you dare wear those swimming!"

"I won't," I mutter while Sam quietly snickers at Mom's chastising.

My best friend flicks a look at me before saying, "I think the customary wedding gift is earrings, actually. I've been reading up on it all to begin building Tristan and Kresley's wedding gift registry."

Mom's hands flutter. "Oh, wonderful idea, Samantha! Thank you for being such a good friend." Of course, she gives props, where there's gifts and money involved.

Stefan lifts my hair from my shoulders, "All right you two hold that talking for a few. Let's get this bleach rinsed out and toned." Handing my now empty drink to Sam, I follow him into the bathroom and the blissful quiet. I need to get myself mentally ready for tonight, and not even a spa and massage package could prepare my mind and body for the crazy evening ahead of me.

Chapter Fourteen

"Ready for tonight?" Cole asks as we wait around for Father to get back from his latest business trip. He rarely cuts them short, but the magnitude of tonight's party will warrant him wanting to be here. Hell, anybody who's anyone important wants to be here.

Sighing, I nod. I don't want to discuss my feelings, especially with my brother. He's been pretty nonexistent when it comes to Kresley, besides crushing on her and keeping her distracted. I'm not complaining, it's what we agreed on from the start, but it doesn't mean I can't be slightly jealous that she seems to be closer to him than me. It's good old-fashioned sibling rivalry, and in this case, I'm not used to losing. Women love me. They love him, too, but they usually flock to me quicker than to him.

Cole doesn't hesitate to call me out. "Bullshit! I heard you in the gym at five a.m."

My eyes fly to his. "You were up?"

He shrugs. "Couldn't sleep. I'm used to you being in there during football season, but not that early in your off time."

Raking my hand over my face, I release a breath and agree. He's right. Brent and I work out together most times, but it's Christmas vacation. When we're on break, we hit the gym later than our usual four a.m. before school training sessions. "Yeah, I didn't sleep much either."

"Is it beba?"

"Yep," I admit, taking a drink of the piping hot black coffee. Our head housekeeper makes the best coffee I've ever tasted. Not sure how she does it, but the stuff works miracles on hangovers. "I'm starting to like her," I admit and he snorts.

"You think? Pretty sure we all like her."

"I know. I wasn't expecting it to be this confusing though. Feelings in the past have always been fleeting, but with her, it's the opposite. That's unsettling, to be honest."

"What exactly? That you desire to actually be with her, versus just putting on another show to make dad proud?"

"Exactly."

"It's not only you, Tris. You're not alone. We all want her more than usual, even Brent. I see it in the podnas eyes when he looks at her. This started as one thing, but it's changing, ya' know?"

When he's laid-back or pissed, his accent is more pronounced. It makes me miss home. "So what am I supposed to do, go through with everything tonight and not skip a beat or question it?"

"Of course. Everything is still the same until dad says differently."

Giving in, I readily agree. I already know how it is, but I needed to hear him say it too—the reassurance. "I have to find Axel," I mutter and take my coffee with me to the indoor pool. If my brother's not reading, drawing, or whatever else it is that smart people do, he's swimming. With the party happening tonight, he'll be trying to swim some of his anxiety out beforehand.

"Ax," I call out loud enough it echoes in the room. At least he'll be able to hear me while he finishes his lap and is distracted.

Coming to a stop at the edge nearest me, he bob's in the massive, deep, heated pool. "Yes?" His hands rake over his face swiping away the stray water droplets. "You're up early. I wasn't expecting you for a couple more hours."

With a shrug, I explain, "I was up early and hit the gym."

"Right," he murmurs aware it's how I tend to process heavy topics.

"Anything changing that I should know about?"

"Uh, you mean for tonight?"

"Yes, for the party."

"No, just try and enjoy the festivities. It'll go smoother if you relax and lay the charm on strongly. So far, everything's still going to plan."

"Fine...has Kresley said anything to you?"

"About what?" Axel heads for the pool stairs and climbs out of the water. He grabs his towel to toss over his shoulder. He's as tall as my brothers and me, but he's slim, with a lightly corded physique. His form's nearly the opposite of my hard, jacked-up muscles, and I can't help but wonder which body type Kresley prefers more.

"Just forget it." I huff as he reaches for his glasses, the kid can't see much up close. Planting them in place, he meets my stare.

"No, let's discuss this. What's going on with you? I'm not accustomed to you being so unsure about anything, and that's the vibe rolling of you. Neither Kresley nor anyone else tonight can be made aware that you're questioning things."

"I wasn't expecting to like her," I admit, my palms rubbing against my thighs as I decide to confide in him.

Cole's lips turn up, pleased. He confesses, "I don't believe any of us were, to be honest. The first day she was pretty rude and then she took her time in getting comfortable with us, especially you and Brent. Considering how much we're around her, it's a good thing we like her," he finishes with a chuckle.

"I know smartass. It's just a lot of pressure with the party tonight."

He nudges the corner of his glasses. "It'll be fine. You handle pressure the best out of all of us. This is your domain, brother, being in the spotlight."

"If you say so."

He shoots me a look. "Just take it in stride Tristan, as you usually do. Kresley is quiet, but she'll be perfect tonight by your side. You'll see."

"Thanks, man," I slap his shoulder, and he winces. I guess I shouldn't smack him that hard when his skin's wet. *Oh well.*

"The real struggle will be getting Brent in a tux."

"You know as well as I do that he'll show up semicasual in some type of a sport coat."

"If that happens, Father will lose it on him; we've seen it happen before."

"Might be entertaining," I snicker with a shrug.

"Not with the sharks swimming so closely. The five of us need to be a united front; we need to seem smooth and impenetrable."

"We will," I assure him. "You always steer us on the right path. It's why Father discusses so much business with you and not the rest of us."

His cheeks grow pink, and I huff a laugh as I head for my room. I may as well attempt to take a nap while I wait for our father and his latest sidepiece pretending to be my next mommy to eventually arrive. Too bad she can't take the hint. Our mother died during our birth, we'll never want or need another to fill her spot. Especially not one who is only five years older than my brothers and me. Fuck that!

Brent

"I look like an uptight dipshit," I grumble as Father's team works at getting us all presentable for the party. Staring at my hair in the massive mirror, I run my hands through the stiff gel, messing it up a bit. The personal stylist tried making my hair look like Dad's, which is not the way I like it. I prefer the messy look, kind of how my moods are when dealing with stupid people.

"You look good," Tristan argues. Axel and Cole both nod with agreement, but I still don't care.

"I hate these things," I complain, throwing my hands up. "My arms never fit right; I'm going to pop the damn stitches." I continue to nag and gain Father's attention.

"If they aren't comfortable, then you need to get them retailored."

A shudder rocks through me at the thought of being poked, prodded, and measured. It makes me feel like a gorilla in a tea shop how they always hmm and haw about my overly toned body. I play sports and get in the occasional fist fight; being in shape is the only way I know how to be, and they want to put me in suits like a fucking stuffed sausage.

"I'm good." I protest and turn to leave. This is a bunch of bullshit; we don't really need these people dressing us anyhow. We're men; all we should need is a jacket, deodorant, and a dime-size amount of gel. I can read the damn directions; it doesn't take all this extra to be presentable.

"Relax son." Dad grins. "You go through with tonight, and you boys can take the jet to Aspen and ski for the next week. Have some fun, meet a few girls and enjoy your holiday break."

Meeting girls is the last thing on my mind. I have Kresley. Skiing does sound like fun, though, especially if we're going to have to put up with a ton of nosey people tonight. "All right," I easily concede, feeling better knowing I'll get to do something I enjoy in the next few days. "A trip sounds good."

Dads smile grows, and he turns to speak to Axel, effectively cutting me out of their conversation like usual.

Tristan sighs and tilts his head toward the doorway, "Let's go out there and eat before it gets any later. I won't get a chance to have anything to eat tonight with all the people."

Tristan's like me. If we don't get to eat, we get punchy. The last time it happened, Dad had to sue and bankrupted the people pissing my brother and me off. If anything, it taught us to be prepared. When we aren't, Father likes to ruin lives like it's his sport of choice. Not that I care much about anyone else. I've learned the hard way not to; they all only want us for money and status anyhow. Rarely do we meet someone with any real substance, without an ulterior motive in their back pocket.

Except Kresley. The thought creeps in my mind, and I try to immediately shut it down. I can't think of her like that right now. Tonight is only about her and Tristan and the plan falling into place like we've mapped out.

"I want to take her with us," I burst, as soon as we enter the vast kitchen. Each surface is overtaken with platters of neatly positioned foods, along with various other delicious looking items to be put out for the party tonight. The chef and her hired assistants are manning the stove and countertops like they haven't a second to waste. With the amount of guests coming, they probably don't have any extra time to screw off.

Tristan leans in and quietly probes, "What are you babbling about? You can't sprout off random shit and expect me to read your mind."

With a hungry, irritated sigh, I mutter, "We're quads, and after so many years, you'd think we'd be able too."

"No kidding. Now, what are you talking about?"

"Father said we can take the jet to Aspen."

"Yeah, I was there, remember?"

"I'm going to break your nose. Stop being a dick because you're anxious for tonight. It'll only get you decked. Now, what I meant was that I want to bring Kresley along with us if we decide to leave town. I don't like the idea of her being near her father or selfish mother without us to protect her if needed."

"Ah, you'll miss her..." He breaks it down.

My shoulders bounce in a noncommittal shrug, not wanting to admit jackshit.

"Why are you too stubborn to come out and say that you like her? You practically ignore her all the time, yet if anyone looks at her, you throttle them for it. You can say it out loud to me, Brent. You're aware that we all have feelings for her."

"I don't share this stuff; you're aware of that more so than anyone, Tris."

"Yeah, but maybe you should take a stab at it and start. We all need to be on the same page, especially when it comes to Kresley. I think it'll be a good idea to have some time away from her. We're getting a little too close and attached to her."

With a growl, I state, "Fuck it, then I'll stay home." Reaching for the first vegetable item I see, I shove some broccoli florets in my mouth and chew angrily. I'm hungry, but not about to jack up my diet by eating the pastries and other empty carb appetizers spread out around us. Processed sugars are the damn devil when it comes to detoxing it back out. Cole, however, eats it all like he has no care in the world, which is fine—for him.

Tristan grabs for a crab cake, and I bat his hand toward the steamed shrimp. He'd be the size of the house if I didn't pay attention to what he's always grabbing for. We have a nutritionist yet you'd think Tris never learned a thing over the years of playing ball. If he eats any crap, he'll be tossing his guts in the morning when he works out.

"No, you won't," he argues and chucks a jumbo-sized shrimp into his mouth. After he chews and swallows, he continues, "Cole and Axel will want her with us too. She can come. Our ski bunnies will be disappointed we won't want to play with any of them though. You can't tell me you won't miss the s'more blow jobs."

Rolling my eyes, I spear some asparagus and take a big bite. The bacon and butter wrapped vegetable taste explodes over my tongue. Our chef is an insane cook. She can take anything healthy and make it taste sinfully good. "As long as I can teach Kresley how to ski, I won't need any other females around. She's worth far more than a cheap, fucking BJ." He wants me to be upfront with my feelings, then so be it. If he runs his mouth, I'll make good on my promise to break his nose.

"It's settled then. While we're at it, we may as well have the place decorated and everything for her. I'll call ahead and make sure they put up a tree along with the decorations out before we arrive. You want to pick up some gifts for her there or wait until we're back? I'm assuming it'll be our best time to celebrate a private Christmas with her."

"I want to spoil her."

"She won't care about that stuff, Brent. You're well aware of how she is. She's not like those other girls who want us to drop a load of money on them and flash them to whoever will notice."

"It's one of the reasons I like her."

He nods and agrees. "I know man; me too."

It's settled. We'll get through the big production of tonight. I'll ask Dad to talk to Kresley's parents, so she's allowed to come with us without any hassle. We'll leave town and have a quiet week with just the five of us. Dad never wants to go, so we don't have to worry about him. I couldn't think of a better way to spend my holiday break than with my best friends and the girl that's starting to steal our hearts.

Chapter Fifteen

Kresley

"For the hundredth time, stop fidgeting!" Mom scolds. I beam a fake smile in return and allow Axel to take my hand. He leads me away a few steps.

"You looked like you needed to be saved," he confesses so only I can hear.

"You have no idea. I could kiss you for it."

"Hold that thought." He takes off at an even quicker pace, and I have to practically jog to keep up with his stride. It's not an easy feat with the super high shoes that the personal shopper picked out for my dress. Sam did an absolutely fantastic job choosing the style and color of my gown. I swear she needs to select clothes for special events for super famous celebrities. It'd be the perfect job for her. Maybe I can have her do all my outfits once I become Tristan's wife and am in the spotlight like his family always seems to be. That's definitely something I'm not looking forward to.

We round another corner, moving farther away from the ballroom and the guest's bathrooms. Randomly, Axel opens a door and then tugs me inside. "Where are we?" I breathe, with my heart thundering in my chest.

"In a maid's closet," he murmurs, and I let loose a giggle.

"Shit! I don't want any of the staff to hear us!" I whisper laugh. I can't help my excited giggle, though. This is not very Axel like behavior, and I'm secretly thrilled he's decided to hide me away for a bit.

"It's okay, they won't say anything if they see us. They all know to be discreet."

I nod, beaming.

"I had to steal you away before you started dealing with that persistent line of photographers and answering their questions."

"That'll actually happen?" I ask. "I thought we'd take one photo and then everyone would know what this party was about since they got an invitation."

He shakes his head and grins. "You're so cute. Not in here, but Dad has a line of people waiting outside to take a couple photos and ask about all the wedding details."

"Oh, my God!"

"I know." His hand rubs the back of his neck. He cringes and divulges, "He enjoys the stir up, especially since it's good news revolving around our family name."

"It's overwhelming," I admit, and he agrees.

"It's exactly why I came to steal you away, my Lois Lane."

"Oh?"

He nods, moving his hands to my waist. "I've thought of you all day," he reveals, stepping closer. The tips of our shoes touch and he leans in, nudging my nose with his. It's cute, and my smile grows.

"You promise?"

"Mm-hmm." He moves to nuzzle my neck, peppering sweet,

soft kisses along my throat and under my ear. It feels fantastic, his warm breath and silky tongue bringing chills to my flesh. I squirm in his arms, and he chuckles, pulling me against his sturdy frame.

"Axel," I sigh. He moves his face, so his lips are hovering over mine, our breaths mingling. These boys drive my mind and body insane, especially when we're alone like this. "Kiss me, Axel."

"Say please," he murmurs, his voice going thick and raspy with lust.

"Please," I murmur barely audible, but it does the trick.

He tilts his head a touch, his lips descending on mine. He kisses me with such pent-up desire it has my head completely spinning. A moan escapes, and he takes advantage, diving in and kissing me deeper. Not only is he brilliant, but he's sweet and talented with his mouth.

Axel's everything in a boy I could possibly ever want. The only problem is that I want his brothers just as fiercely and that's so confusing. Our tongues duel as his hands hold me to him like his life depends on it. His lips are plump and taste like mint. He's skipped the drinks and stuck to water if I'd have to guess. He's the responsible brother out of the four and always aware of everything. Cole's the reckless one, drinking the liquor while Brent broods in a corner and Tristan dazzles the crowd with his bright smile and charm. Together, they make an overwhelming force, and also too hard to give up.

My skin ignites as my breasts suddenly seem more cumbersome and feel swollen in the push-up bra I'm wearing. I have so many things going on at once, I don't know what to do or what to ask him for. "Axel," I moan. "I need..." I trail off, and he groans with his own desire.

"Jesus, I want you. You taste so good, Kresley—like peaches, and you smell like flowers."

Grinning against his lips, I disclose the reasoning behind both. "It's the wine and my perfume."

"Well, it's making me want to taste you everywhere."

"Yes," I sigh, and he drops to his knees.

His movement catches me off guard and my brow hikes, "Axel? What are you?" I get cut off as his hands go under my long dress. His fingers graze against my skin, pushing my legs apart. I'm staring down at him dumbstruck as his hands pause on the insides of my thighs. My gown is hiked up far enough he can easily see the scrap of panties I'm wearing.

"Perfect," he croons and leans in. His nose presses into my sensitive button as he inhales. A whimper escapes me as intense sparks shoot throughout my body.

"Wow, that's just wow..."

"I want to taste you," he rasps, and I nearly choke on air.

"O-okay," I stammer, not entirely sure of what he plans to do next. I certainly wasn't expecting him to lick over the front of my lace panties before moving them aside. "Oh fuck," I breathe as his mouth lands on my clit. This is entirely new territory for me, so when he begins to suck, my hand flies over my mouth to keep me from screaming. Holy fuck that feels amazing! "Ax-Ax-Axelll," I plea, as my eyes remain trained on his head between my thighs. It's seriously the sexiest thing I've ever seen.

"Mm," he hums and then does this light nibble thing with his teeth. Whatever it is, the move has sensations washing over me from top to bottom, inside and out. My core throbs with zings of pleasure, wetness gushes between my thighs, and then I'm shifting around, attempting to widen my legs as much as possible. I want to shove his face into my hot, needy core but I wouldn't dare do it unless he told me to.

"Oh my God, please!" I whimper, not above begging him for more.

He presses a digit into my entrance, and the long, thick finger makes my center contract around the welcome intrusion. He's sucking, nibbling and fingering me so rough and dirty and it's too much for my body and mind to process. With a few thrusts of his finger, I'm exploding. A powerful orgasm slams into me. He pumps his finger in and out, slurping at my juices as I shake and quietly whimper through the release. It's tough to be quiet while he's sending me spiraling, full of pleasure.

He stands up, licking his lips and adjusting the impressive length in his slacks. It's more than noticeable in the thin material. I want to unzip the trousers and free him, I want to feel just how big he really is.

"That was-that was...wow. I don't know what to say," I admit and he grins, eyes sparkling with delight. "Thank you, you're pretty amazing."

"You taste delicious. Both sets of your full lips are sweet, my Lois."

My body flushes all over again at his confession.

"You're really good at, um, that," I admit, my cheeks feeling like they're on fire, but I can't find it in me to care at the moment. He completely shocked me by stealing me away, hiding me in a closet and then proceeding to kiss me in multiple places. There's no way I was expecting him to offer up such an intense orgasm either.

Axel chuckles and pulls my frame to his again. He places a soft, chaste kiss on my mouth before moving away to readjust my dress. His deft fingers move it back in place for me, and I can only stand still and watch him with rapt attention. "You're breathtaking, in more ways than one tonight. I want you to remember that through everything, okay?"

I nod, pleased with his praise and the sincerity behind it. "Thank you, not only for saying that but also for tonight. For bringing me in here with you and making me feel special."

"You are special to me—to all of us." He wraps me tightly in his warm, loving embrace one last time, then tugs me back out into the hallway and back to reality.

Following along, I can't help but be paranoid that everyone knows what we were up to. Axel must notice my fidgeting and unease because he stops next to the ladies bathroom and gestures to the door. "Go freshen up and if anyone questions you, I was simply you fortunate bathroom escort."

"Okay." I flash a thankful smile and peck his cheek before quickly rushing into the ladies room.

I'm positively giddy inside. I can't believe all of that just happened between us. I mean holy shit! Never in a million years would I have imagined that Axel could do that thing with his mouth. Is it wrong that I'm now wondering if the other three know how to do the same as well? I don't even want to think about how they've learned to do it. Looking at Axel you'd think he'd be more reserved and…well…less experienced. Obviously, I have no idea what I'm talking about here.

I finish cleaning myself up. The entire time I can't stop from reminiscing how Axel had sucked and nibbled on my private parts. It feels like he's still there in a sense, barely grazing my flesh. God, I can't wait to do that again, that much is for sure. Washing my hands, my irises flick over my reflection, and remarkably, I look just as expected. My face is a bit rosy, my eyes sparkling, and lips a bit swollen, but otherwise, I'm pretty much put together, thankfully. Good thing Axel had the sense to briefly fix my dress and everything; I was too flabbergasted to even consider it.

Tossing the paper towel into the trash bin, I make my way back into the hall only to find the man of the hour gone. Brent stands stoically, arms crossed over his chest in his signature brooding manner, in Axel's place. "Oh!" I exclaim, my hand fluttering to my chest. I wasn't expecting to see him here and now. "Hi!" I offer a smile.

"Hm," he rumbles. Brent's lazy gaze takes me in slowly from the top of my expertly styled hair down to my hand-crafted stilettos. His tongue darts over his bottom lip before finishing, "Ax had to go help." He tilts his chin in the direction heading toward the ballroom. He's such a man's man, grunting a few words and expecting me to fill in the rest.

"Okay, no problem." My smile evens out a bit, and I step closer to the big guy leaning against the wall. In the beginning, I never would've approached him so easily, but I've warmed up to his briskly temperature. I know it's not me at all; it's just his personality. He's the protector, the rough one out of the quads. "And you just so happened to wait out here for me?"

Brent shrugs his massive shoulders, the edge of his luscious, full lips tilting upward into a playful smirk. "Maybe."

My brow rises, and my mouth drops in mock surprise, my hand fluttering to my chest as I mock their Southern drawl. "Brent de Lacharriere, the gentleman. What will people think when they find out the truth about you?" I tease, feeling braver after being intimate with Axel.

Brent shakes his head in amusement. With a sigh, he stands to his full height, towering over me easily. His closeness makes me feel warm all over again. He also smells insanely good, like man and soap and his pheromones are off the wall with how much he works out. I swear it's like he has a giant magnet just drawing me to him. He could be a complete dick and ignore absolutely everyone, yet his presence alone is alluring.

"Who says my intentions are gentlemanly?" he murmurs, his deep voice coating me like thick molasses. Sometimes I even break out in chills when I hear him talk. Brent oozes sex appeal in everything he does, and the kicker is that he doesn't realize it. Or maybe he does, and he just doesn't care. Whatever the case may be, I can't seem to be around him enough to have my fill.

My hands fall to his wide, muscular chest, taking in his rock-solid form. "Show me then," I whisper in a confidently masked plea.

The champagne I've been drinking must be making me braver than usual because I'm never so blunt with Brent. The both of us prefer to dance around each other. I pretend to be aloof to my not-so-accidental touches when it comes to him, and eventually, he loses patience. He'll become angry and get in my face, and then he'll chastise me for something and nearly kiss me. That's how it works between us; it's our silent dance of wills. He's held off from kissing me, but I'm beginning to wonder if he's doing it on purpose to torment us both. The anticipation of his mouth on mine is starting to drive me insane whenever I'm around him, and it's all I seem to be able to think about.

Unwelcome voices interrupt our privacy in the hallway, and I take a casual step back, removing my hands from his body. This night is about Tristan and me, after all. If I'm caught in a compromising position, people probably won't understand, even if the quads know I'm like this with each of them. Three women make their way around the corner to where we are, flashing fake smiles in our direction. I don't know who they are, but that's not surprising. I barely know anyone here. The guest list wasn't something I had access to either, aside from being able to request that a few be sent to my family and Sam.

Brent holds his elbow out to me as etiquette has taught him over the years. He's so buff compared to his three other brothers that it makes him seem taller than the others somehow. Placing my hand in the crook of his arm, I allow him to carefully lead me back toward the ballroom and away from the nosey ladies. I'm sure they wouldn't hesitate to spread gossip around, and I refuse to be the one to embarrass the de Lacharrieres.

As we're stepping into the busy room full of orchestra music, polite conversation, and subdued laughter, Brent leans in close. His lush lips lightly brush against the tender flesh of my earlobe, and I shiver with the gentle caress. He gravelly rasps, sending the best kind of shivers and goosebumps over me. "One day we won't get interrupted, sweetheart. I hope you're prepared for what I'll do to you, to your body." With that intense, sexually charged promise, he moves his arm from my grip and strides away. In his wake, he leaves a trail of delicious cologne to mock me. I want to chase after him and make him keep his word, but we both know that can't happen right now.

My heart's beating so fast...my stomachs full of flickering nerves and my core's throbbing with desire all over again. Brent's the dangerous brother; I don't doubt that for even a minute. He's the strong, silent type that doesn't allow anything to stand in the way of what he wants. All this sexy, sweet torment is mere foreplay to him, getting us both completely overwhelmed with pent-up need. When he leaves me with promises like that, and he does it often, I can't help but wish for the day it finally happens. I have a feeling that when Brent eventually gives in to his desires, he'll gain more than my body; he'll claim my heart and soul as well.

Chapter Sixteen

My feet are absolutely killing me in these crazy high heels from standing and dancing all evening, so I eventually escape. Leaving behind all the commotion of the party, I go in search of a place to rest not only my feet but my overworked head. I wouldn't exactly label me as an introvert, but I'm definitely not an extrovert. I'm somewhere in the middle and being around so many people can be a bit overpowering.

The photos and questions seemed intense at times, but Tristan reassured me on multiple occasions that I handled it all well. I can't believe he's the one stuck in the limelight all the time along with his father. He took everything in stride, flashing his perfect white smile for the pictures and even going as far as to charm the paparazzi. I can understand why the country seems to adore him. No one has witnessed the real version of Tristan like I have, and I have a feeling the de Lacharrieres work hard to keep it that way. He's a total bullheaded asshole when you first meet him. He gets what he wants, and he'll do whatever's needed to make sure it happens, no matter the repercussions.

However, after all that, I've been lucky enough to observe another side to him as well. He's extremely loyal when it comes to his family, and in my case, me. Once he proposed, I was in the fold with his family as far as he's concerned. Tristan's never questioned the engagement or me, and now I can see what I was utterly blind to when we first met.

Tristan has a massive drive, too; he sets his sights on something and puts his all into it. When the girls at school became jealous and started to push their weight around with me, he had me with him at lunch daily. He figured out a way to step in, but he did it in his own way. Going to the cheerleaders eventually wasn't what I'd have done personally, but once I took his advice and made my presence known with the squad, the mean girls backed off. Tristan may come off as single-minded to many, but that's not the case at all. He has so many concerns he's silently working through that he never lets on about until he's ready for you to know. I guess he's similar to Axel in that sense.

Maybe a future linked to Tristan won't be so bad after all. Not that I have much choice in the matter, but with him warming up to me and being kinder, I've slowly been tearing my walls down. I've been falling for him bit by bit, not like the plunge feeling I was expecting from love. Maybe it's different in this sense because I've become enraptured with the four de Lacharriere brothers, rather than with only one man. This thing with Tristan feels stronger than just a blind love. It's like we're both feeling each other out and gaining a mutual respect for the other, along with wanting to be around one another more as the days pass and our trust has a chance to blossom.

Axel may have swept me off my feet first with his friendship and kind disposition, but I can understand why our fathers have matched Tristan and me. He'll make a good, strong husband that can handle anything thrown at us. I have my own strength inside and together we'd be like a steel beam when faced with mutual adversary or whatever the case may be. Tristan reminds me of a prince really, stuck in his ivory tower and conforming to what he's been taught, as well as doing what's expected of him. He takes everything that's handed to him, twists it until he makes it work, and lets it grow from there.

I have to find the greatness in his sacrifice and respect him for it as I hope he'll do the same with me. Tristan may not always be agreeable or the kindest of the bunch, but with his father, I can understand why he is the way he is. After all, look at my father and what I've become because of him. I'm strong inside with a determination to do better, not financially, but as a human being.

I want to share my feelings with the quads, but I wonder if maybe it's too soon. I know they like me. They've all kissed me except for Brent, but he's almost kissed me nearly every day. I still don't understand what's holding him back, but the tension building between us is driving me crazy. I'm far past wanting him to only kiss me; at this point, I want him to consume me.

Would it be corny if I used Christmas to admit to the guys that I'm falling in love with them? The more intimate we become, the harder it is for me to hold back. I've never felt so confused or strongly about anyone before, and it's not just one of them, but all of them. I don't know what I'll do about my feelings for each of the boys when Tristan and I finally marry. I shouldn't call them boys anymore; they're looking more like full-grown men with each passing day. It's easy for me to forget they're a year older than me since we're all in the same grade.

Cole tells me not to worry, but how can I possibly not think about it sometimes? How can I just sit back while I fall further in love with each of them? I have to say something. They deserve to know the truth: that I don't think I could ever choose between them. *I love them.* The feeling plows into me like a ton of bricks. The revelation is trivial, yet essential all in the same sense.

My thoughts are interrupted by approaching voices. "We can speak in here, Father," Tristan's dad says to the guys' grandfather.

I was shocked when the senior Mr. de Lacharriere showed up tonight. I had no idea he was planning to come to the party, and everyone was vying to get the uber wealthy man's attention. It has to be hard being as rich as he is with money-grubbing vultures always flocking around. I'm sure that's what his brisk attitude is from as well. I was expecting a warm welcome from the man much like Tristan's dad, but that wasn't the case at all. The botoxed gramps had practically snubbed his nose at me when I went in for a hug rather than a quick, polite, fake cheek kiss. Maybe that's where Brent's grumpiness evolved from.

I don't know why, but I hop off the couch I'd found to rest my feet on, not wanting the men to see me sitting alone in the library. I would make my presence known, but my gut tells me not to. I'm sure they'd find it suspicious if I'm wandering alone though the mansion during a lavish party. Tristan's dad may be nice, but I'm not so sure how he'd react if he thought I was snooping or something.

The door opens just as I wedge myself behind a display case. Luckily, only the top and front portion is glass. The rest of the shelf is an intricately-carved, mahogany wood lined in thick, emerald velvet. It probably cost a fortune, and it's just sitting here tucked away and forgotten in a room I doubt anyone regularly uses. Regardless, it becomes my impromptu hiding spot.

Holding my breath for a moment, I hear the massive door click shut and the men's steps quieted by the round Turkish rug with filigree edges that take up a good portion of the floor. Whoever designed the room has made it feel like you can come in anytime and tuck into a couch and simply read the day away. I could only dream of ever owning something like this myself. Though with Tristan's wealth and taste, there's no telling what kind of house we'll have or where we'll live. I wouldn't be surprised if he plans to have multiple homes in many cities like his father does.

"Would you care for a drink, Father?"

"Whiskey," the older man acknowledges, and glass clinks as the ice is chucked inside and the liquor is poured into expensive tumblers. Peeking around the corner, I watch as he hands the glass off and both men take a seat on the couch I'd vacated only minutes prior. "Now, explain to me what's with this girl? I looked into her; she has nothing of substantial worth. Her family's well-heeled, but nowhere near the level of our own prosperity. Why would you marry your most promising son off to someone without anything to offer our legacy?" he asks, and Tristan's father flashes a wicked smile in return.

His comment hurts, I won't lie about that. It digs a little deep as I'm always seen as a mere ticket value and nothing more. But, I was also expecting it with this family, so I've sort of prepared myself. Or so I thought I had, as the dig scratches a bit too severely into my self-eradicated armor. In all honesty, I was anticipating the press to ask this and splatter whatever they dreamed up in the tabloids. The simple fact that it's a private conversation held between Tristan's father and grandfather, well, I can manage to live with it.

"When my staff drew up the files on the neighbors around our temporary house, I discovered something about her father. Or, I should actually recognize that it was the boys who found it."

"Oh?"

The younger version nods and says, "Her father has a company, and after looking it over, I want it."

"And the engagement?"

"It's a well-planned distraction. This nonsense party and the various announcements buy me time while her father unknowingly hands over enough access to information for me to take it. I'll liquidate everything as soon as possible, and my bank account will grow as his disperses."

The grandfather chuckles with glee. "It's quite the farce, and the boys are invested as well?"

"Oh, without a doubt. This is the fifth job they've helped me cultivate. I'm training them very well to take over my company in due time. This entire plan was actually Axel's idea. He's the one who looked over her file and let me know that a few months of a charade could pay off so handsomely."

I'm in shock. Like, I have no idea what to do or how to act with this newly-discovered information. My muscles are clenched tight, and my heart's on the cusp of shattering into a million jagged shards. Breathless, I make myself remain still and take in every single horrific detail of my family's planned demise.

"Axel believes that by the end of the year we'll have everything we need to complete the takeover."

"And next year? I thought this academy was important for the boys to graduate from."

"Oh, it is. If you're talking about what happens to the girl, well, they won't have to worry about seeing her again. Her family will be dirt poor. She'll never be able to afford the gas to get there, let alone attend the academy next year. She'll be put in the public-school system, and my boys will have another takeover to notch on their belts and add to their future resumes. They've really embraced this one, too, working together like a well-oiled machine. I've never been prouder."

"I can imagine. You've worked out quite the system, and with the five of you together, the companies will never see you coming. You've become the force, just as I've taught you to be. Good job. Just one more thing..."

"Yes?"

"What if they develop feelings for her? They are impressionable young men, after all. You remember what it was like on the cusp of adulthood, all those raging hormones. You couldn't get your fill of women back then; I can only imagine now."

Tristan's dad laughs outright, jovially confessing, "Very true. They have my permission to toy with her a bit if necessary. I told them to play as much as they want, but she'll never be more than a mistress when it comes down to it. I've warned them of what happens to bastard babies as well, just as you taught me at their age. My boys won't marry for a long while. I want them to enjoy college and women before settling down with lawyers and prenuptial agreements. When the day finally arrives, they'll choose someone who complements our family; that much I can assure you. Maybe it'll be a merger of sorts or who knows what, but they're far too smart than to fall for the nobody daughter from a has-been entrepreneur we choose to destroy."

The grandfather nods with his approval, taking another healthy sip from his tumbler of dark liquor. The men grow quiet, contemplative, for a moment before the heavy door opens again, and the quads stride into the room. Just seeing their faces has my cheeks flushing and my blood boiling. I can't believe they'd ever do something like what their father just divulged. I don't want to believe it. We've grown too close; they can't be completely faking it...right?

"My boys!" their father greets affectionately. "I was just filling your grandfather in on our mutual business plan."

Tristan enters the room, joining the two older men and leans against the arm of the couch his grandfather sits comfortably on before saying, "What did you think of the party, Grandfather?"

The mature man grins, and it transforms his face to look like an older replica of his son and grandsons. The genes in this family are incredibly overpowering with how much they all resemble each other. I bet when the two men were younger, they both looked the same as the quads do now. "You were perfect, as always, grandson."

His gaze falls on Axel as well—the boy who had me in a closet earlier, nearly screaming his name out with pleasure.

I'm beyond mortified for being intimate with Axel and letting him do that to me now. I never should've allowed him to touch me and lick me like he did earlier. It meant nothing to him; it was just another way for the guys to take advantage of me. I'm such a damn fool and to think he was my real friend or that he wanted me in other ways. I'm so stupid and so fucking blind. The worst part is that Axel's the de Lacharriere I've always felt the closest too. He's the one I knew that I loved first and yet, he's also the person who came up with this entire plan to ruin my family and me.

"Axel," his grandfather beams. "Your mind is absolutely brilliant, my boy. You make your father and me proud. This plan that you've concocted seems to be flawless from what your father's been saying."

Axel nods, his cheeks tinging with a touch of pink. "Yes, sir, you're correct. Once I breezed through the background information in the neighbors' files, I'd remembered an article I'd come across months before. It was touching over Kresley's father's company and its many struggles. They were seeking potential investors to help lighten the burden so they could overcome their issues."

He continues, going in depth with their plans. "The five of us then begun to invest under our individual LLC's. Throughout the year, we'll continue to buy up a small portion, enough to dig our fingers into the core information at least. They have a baseline before you're allowed access to specific files and client information. We should have everything we need by the spring to inflict a takeover completely. Dad will liquidate, and then we move on to the next."

Silent sobs overtake me at hearing him confess. No doubt it's only a small portion of the bigger, in-depth plan they have for my father's company. How could they be so cruel? Everything from day one…from the very beginning was nothing but a cold-hearted lie full of scheming deception, all for the love of money.

Secretly watching them, I can't help but plead in my mind that one of them stands up. I need them to scream that they won't do it, that they've fallen in love with me. That won't happen, however. My wishful thinking is only a sad fairy tale from a blind girl. I know it, just by taking their serious expressions. This was nothing but a convenient job for them while they wrap up their high school education. They'll be unstoppable in college and as adults if they're this deceiving as teenagers.

Cole and Brent remain quiet, standing still as statues with their arms crossed over their chests as the other four men in the room carry on with their scheming ways. Their conversation moves to rake over the minute details, like when they graduate, what colleges they'll attend, and other businesses they may acquire. Eventually, they discuss how their grandfather will leave, going back to France and how he expects the quads to visit in the summer. I guess the girls have been asking for the guys, per his excited boasting. Go figure, they have foreign women waiting to comfort them as well. Could this get any worse? My heart feels like it's been ripped out of my chest cavity.

I'm numb and cold inside. The excitement and love I'd been so enraptured with earlier is fleeting. My emotions have been completely rubbed raw, and I'm ready to bleed at the first sharp object I come in contact with. There's nothing I can do in the moment without drawing attention to myself. I have to squat in the snug spot I'd wedged into, while hot, torturous tears track over my cheeks.

After what seems like forever, Mr. de Lacharriere and the senior de Lacharriere finally say their good-byes and make their exit. With them out of the room, I can no longer remain in my torturous hiding place. I can't be here for another second. I'm ruined, and I refuse for them to have the satisfaction of thinking they've won.

With that thought, I stand from my hiding place.

Chapter Seventeen

"So you found out our original plan," Tristan murmurs with a nonchalant bounce of his broad shoulders. He seems so cold and detached, cruel even, as he notices me standing here. How could he just turn his emotions on and off like that? He was holding and kissing on me not even an hour ago in front of everyone.

I'm shaking and sobbing; full of grief for the boys I'd hopelessly fallen for and have already lost. Or maybe, just maybe, I never had them in the first place. My heart is nonexistent in the moment. There's nothing in my chest anymore; the organ is utterly shattered like a thin sheet of glass.

I knew there had to be ulterior motives from the start but was it all fake with him? And his brothers are the same; I was stupid enough to have given up a piece of my *now* blackened heart to them as well. I can't understand it, that this entire plot was one big lie for them and nothing more. Or, I should say, it was many little white lies and all at my expense.

I was beginning to fall for them—all four of them. And they'd deceived me.

End of Book 1
The conclusion is in *Ugly Dark Truth*

Keep Up With Sapphire

Website:
www.authorsapphireknight.com

BookBub:
https://www.bookbub.com/profile/sapphire-knight

Twitter:
https://twitter.com/sapphireknight3

Instagram:
http://instagram.com/authorsapphireknight

Newsletter:
bit.ly/SKnightNewsletter

Facebook:
https://www.facebook.com/AuthorSapphireKnight

Printed in Poland
by Amazon Fulfillment
Poland Sp. z o.o., Wrocław